Megastorm Miranda

Ted Lamb

Copyright © 2020 Ted Lamb.

All rights reserved. No part of this publication may be reproduced, distributed, or transmitted in any form or by any means, including photocopying, recording, or other electronic or mechanical methods, without the prior written permission of the publisher, except in the case of brief quotations embodied in critical reviews and certain other non-commercial. For permission requests contact the address below.
ISBN: 9798606151653
Any references to historical events, real people, or real places are used fictitiously. Names, characters, and places are such stuff as dreams are made on.

D.E.F. Lamb
21 Arthur Bliss Gardens
Cheltenham GL50 2LN

For Caspar and Sarah

Thanks to Octavia Lamb and Anne Gordon for invaluable editing

Miranda presents herself as a real threat to the British Isles, arriving with a huge storm surge. A similar but long-forgotten combination of storm and tidal flood in the 1600s killed 2,000 people in the South West alone.

Many people find their lives changing profoundly with the new storm's arrival. Climate scientists, politicians, journalists, farmers and fishermen must battle overwhelming forces in this fast-moving drama with frighteningly prophetic overtones.

Contents

Chapter 1..1
Chapter 2..10
Chapter 3..17
Chapter 4..23
Chapter 5..33
Chapter 6..39
Chapter 7..44
Chapter 8..53
Chapter 9..62
Chapter 10..71
Chapter 11..80
Chapter 12..93
Chapter 13..102
Chapter 14..111
Chapter 15..118
Chapter 16..124
Chapter 17..136
Chapter 18..153
Chapter 19..159
Chapter 20..164
Chapter 21..179
Chapter 22..189

The Kraken

Below the thunders of the upper deep,
Far far beneath in the abysmal sea,
His ancient, dreamless, uninvaded sleep
The Kraken sleepeth: faintest sunlights flee
About his shadowy sides: above him swell
Huge sponges of millennial growth and height;
And far away into the sickly light,
From many a wondrous grot and secret cell
Unnumbered and enormous polypi
Winnow with giant fins the slumbering green.
There hath he lain for ages and will lie
Battening upon huge seaworms in his sleep,
Until the latter fire shall heat the deep;
Then once by men and angels to be seen,
In roaring he shall rise and on the surface die.

Alfred Lord Tennyson

Chapter 1

In the middle of a late spring night, two seemingly harmless features in the infra-red satellite-scan displays at the Meteorological Office's HQ in Exeter got quite frisky with one another. The ghostly intertwining images made more sense when computers converted the atmospheric pressure data from space and transmissions from remote ocean buoys into isobar charts – the familiar 'spider webs' of TV weather reports.

Gyrating whirlpools of lines showed that instead of acting in a fairly predictable way, Low Pressure Area B, which had been dithering to the south of Iceland, had put on a growth spurt and developed a quite extraordinary crush on Low Pressure Area A, which was approaching Britain from the Atlantic on the wings of the high altitude Jet Stream. Although initially just a vague squiggle, Low A immediately started to speed up, swelling quickly and – apparently – becoming quite irresistible. Both systems had to meet, at once! They had to embrace, unite under a romantic full moon. Within the space of an hour, with a paroxysm of connubial joy they swirled together to form a truly vast cell of low pressure. A little thrill of delight started to ripple along the tail of this new formation and a strong north-easterly gale sprang to life, rapidly accelerating through stage after stage of the Beaufort Scale. A near-full moon had already tugged half the Atlantic Ocean up towards it in preparation for the year's highest tide a little over a day away, and the growing weather system's roaring hurricane blasted into this mass of heaving, inky-black waters.

Storm Miranda had just been born – Storm Miranda-plus, in fact, because she was shepherding along all that mobile water to create a truly massive tidal surge – a 'megasurge' the like of which had not been experienced in modern times, perhaps more menacing than any tsunami. Miranda had not yet been christened but, surprisingly perhaps for most people, the weather bomb she was about to unleash was not historically unprecedented, echoing as it did a savage, long-forgotten and desperately tragic tidal inundation of 1607 – dubbed at the time 'The Great Flood' – in which more than 2,000 people in England and Wales were drowned along with their animals and businesses.

***

Before Miranda's arrival the weather in Britain had been bad enough. Nobody needed all the rain, at least, not this much of it. The whole of the United Kingdom was saturated, its rivers brimming and spilling into farmland and villages and threatening to cut off whole towns. It was almost as bad as the 'triple whammy' of 2020 which had seen three major storms, Ciara, Dennis and Jorge, hot on each other's heels. Just as then, practically the whole country was on a Met Office amber alert – 'be prepared' – and one or two spots close to red alert – 'take action – danger to life'.

Wales was one of the highest rainfall areas. Here, Owen James, a Powys farmer in the upland part of the River Teme catchment, was woken by the telephone ringing at 2.34am on the night of Miranda's birth. He was unaware of the significance this call would play in the coming drama.

Careful to not disturb his sleeping wife Alice, Owen crept downstairs in his pyjamas and approached the instrument with trepidation. In his experience no good came of calls at this time of night. Was it one of their two daughters, perhaps, in some sort of trouble? Maybe one of his grandchildren sick?

"Yes?"

"Mr James?"

Not a familiar voice. He tried to stifle annoyance.

"Yes."

"Sorry to wake you Mr James. It's John Wiltshire at the Environment Agency Midlands office. The flume station on the stream above you has just gone off-scale and you're on our flood alert list. We thought you ought to know in case you have to move stock."

He wished he had been a little less curt. He thanked the man, politely this time, and went back upstairs to dress quickly. A head appeared from under the covers.

"Owen?"

"Flood alert." He started to put on his clothes. "Not all that surprising the way the stream looked yesterday. I'll maybe have to move the sheep in the top field away from it. I can manage alone. It's only a matter of opening the gate and I've got the dog. They'll go straight through it and up to the wood edge. They'll be safe there. Back in no time."

But Alice James sat up anyway, shook her hair and rubbed the sleep out of her dark eyes.

"I'll have some tea ready for when you come back," she said, smiling. They were used to being a team, after all, just like in the lambing season.

As Owen went out into the rainswept yard Meg, his sheepdog, came out of her hay bed in the barn, crouched low, cautious. It was an unexpectedly early wakening and the collie was unsure what was afoot, but once she saw her master heading for the Land Rover her tail wagged furiously and she bounded up, reading his mind perfectly, gave the heels of his wellingtons each a playful nip and then launched herself over the tailgate of the vehicle in one smooth movement. An adventure! Something afoot!

Owen made his way round the vehicle. Reaching for the door handle, he was surprised to feel something flop suddenly onto his right foot. He shone the torch down, frowning, just in time to see a small olive-green creature spring away: a frog.

He climbed in and started the engine. Letting it have a moment or two to warm up he looked back at the dog's face, half white half black, and her quick eyes.

"I don't know what you're so goddam pleased about," he said.

Meg's tail just wagged all the more furiously.

Owen drove the vehicle over to the barn door and left the engine running while he threw three bales of hay in the back beside Meg – his animals would no doubt be grateful for some dry food. Then he set off.

Nosing out of the yard, the lane looked pretty wet, with deep puddles on both sides. That was only to be expected given the intensity of the rain lately, but there was another surprise as he got underway – more frogs. His headlights picked them out, one after another, crossing the road in long hops, some far apart, some in little groups. In spring there was often a frog migration to a dammed section of the smaller stream in the valley off to the right, but by now the spawning season was long over. And these frogs were all heading in the opposite direction, uphill, up the steep sides of the valley in the direction of the ridges. There must have been hundreds of them in the two mile drive to the brookside field gate, of all sizes from inch-long froglets to gangly mums and dads. He had to concentrate hard to avoid running any of them over, but there was no way of telling if any jumped under the wheels. He hoped not, for they were harmless creatures.

The automatic alarm activated by the flume station meant the stream was probably over its bank already. Now that rivers were monitored by these devices, flood conditions were much easier to predict. Flood alerts could then be issued if appropriate. What would happen next depended on how much more rain fell out of the sky. The last big flood had been 2007, a disaster all the way down from Owen's section of stream to the River Teme not far beyond his land, and on down into the already-overloaded River Severn, then down, down, down again all the way to the broad Severn estuary and the sea. Gloucestershire, the last county in line, had fared the worst. The water treatment works at Mythe, just outside Tewkesbury, had been inundated, turning domestic water foul and unusable. Nearby towns including Cheltenham and Gloucester had had to rely on bottled water and trucked-in supplies until the situation was resolved. In Gloucester, a major electricity grid switchgear station had come within inches of being submerged, and those already suffering from water shortages would have had power failure to cope with as well. These were major communities, and although people on the whole behaved well there was talk of profiteering on bottled water and looting from abandoned homes and businesses. Lawlessness, it seemed, was only just under the surface in Britain, civilisation at best notional in some quarters.

Sure, it had rained hard enough back then, but other contributory factors could well be blamed for the disaster. The vast Severn-Teme-Warwickshire Avon river system had historically been well able to look after itself at most times by laying aside excess water in broad, low-lying riverside fields – the area generally known as the flood plain. But bit by bit in recent years, with growing frequency and size, housebuilding projects had bitten into these areas and diminished them greatly.

The homes and the infrastructure that went with them, roads and so on, were laced with efficient drainage networks to speed away any storm water straight into the river. When those storms came the river received all this water in a rush and had little choice but to rise and go on rising.

Owen had no idea how badly the stream banks had been breached until he reached the field where his late-lambers were. At this point the valley edges closed in steeply. He drew into the roadside gateway and got out with his torch, leaving the vehicle's engine ticking over and the headlights burning down towards the rushing water for additional illumination. At first glance things didn't look too good.

Since foot and mouth struck a few years back, he kept only a few animals now, little hardy Welsh Specklefaces, and there ought to have been eight ewes in the field and eight lambs, a pair of twins and four singles (two of the ewes had not produced that year, which was better in a way than losing lambs for other reasons). Sweeping the torch around from the gateway, he first saw a tight knot of sheep on the far side of the swollen river that was coursing along the valley floor and dividing the field in two. Although there was sloping dry ground behind the animals, and they were under the shelter of a waterside spinney to one side, they were bleating loudly, clearly highly concerned – the ladies always kept an eye out for each other, including any offspring.

Packed together as they were, sheep and lambs, it was impossible to count them, just as it was impossible to see what was alarming them – the river alone was no threat and they could easily move away from it. Then he saw what it was. Something moved among the waterside tussocks on his side of the racing stream. It was a lamb, wet, small and shivering. An anxious ewe on one side, a frightened and no doubt very cold and hungry lamb on the other ... not a good recipe. Pretty soon the lamb or its mother would try to pluck up enough courage to take the plunge, but with the state of the water that would be disastrous for either of them, perhaps even both of them. Quickly he shone his torch along the watercourse to the stone bridge that linked the two sides of the stream and saw with a sinking heart that it had all but disappeared. Reputed to have been Roman in origin, only the very central part of the foot-high stone parapet now showed above the surface of the racing water, which would mean at least a foot to wade through in the middle over the top of the bridge arch, with two and a half feet perhaps of quieter water to either side. The main current plunged through the restricting arch to emerge, boiling furiously, on the other side. He'd taken a Land Rover over that bridge before now – you could just squeak across if you were careful with scarcely any space between the low parapets – but in these conditions, with deepish water to either side and the bridge itself under pressure and perhaps destabilised, it would be folly. It would also come well over the top of his wellington boots ... but if that's what had to be done, so be it. He'd been wet and cold before in this job. Taking a trusted blackthorn crook from the Land Rover he was over the gate in one bound and setting off towards the marooned lamb, Meg quickly at his heels after belly-crawling under the gate.

"Look to it Meg, look to it!"

He raised his stick to direct the dog downstream, in the other direction, to see if there were any more marooned animals. Squelching his way to the frightened lamb he picked it up, even though it put on a fair bit of weight since birth, and cradled it. With a little warm milk inside it and a few licks from mum, it would be all right. He was being watched by the little gallery of speckly faces on the far bank – they had all now fallen silent apart from a few little anxious lamb bleats. He was well aware that they all knew him – he had after all helped to bring most of them into the world – but it was still quite impossible to see if the rest of the flock was complete because the attentive ewes kept changing places, like a confusing game of Find the Lady, while their lambs ran this way and that between their legs.

As he set off for the bridge, the flock followed on the other bank, faces all still turned his way. When he plunged into the flood towards them across the top of the bridge they grouped together, a welcoming party, one of them standing ahead of the rest with her forelegs in the water – that was certainly the lamb's mother.

As he had suspected, the water at the side of the bridge had no real force, but it soon came over the tops of his boots. Owen kept on, prodding ahead with his stick to find the depth and wading steadily as he felt the ground rising into the arch. At the top, however, although there was still no pressure, the bridge was vibrating under his feet, an eerie feeling, and he could hear a deep drumming sound from the water rushing beneath it as he reached its crown. The racing water each side now made him feel dizzy, so he tried not to look at it and just kept walking steadily ahead. On the downside he was again in deep water, but all was well, with the ewe coming further in to meet him then backing a bit as he drew near. He shooed her back and lowered the lamb on dry land under her nose. She had barely sniffed at it before a loud crack made them both start, man and sheep. It came from the riverbank by the spinney where he had first seen the animals. Owen swept the torch beam round to illuminate a large tree-trunk writhing in midstream, restrained by the three strands of barbed wire strung bank-to-bank to keep the animals out of the spinney, which was on his upstream neighbour's ground. It was a pollarded willow, but there was something odd about it and for some seconds he could not determine what that something was until he realised it had its roots in the air – it was upside down! As he watched, the huge thing gave a sudden jolt – one of the wires had given way. He watched, rooted with horrified fascination, while another strand gave, and the monster bucked and twisted even more. This spooked the other sheep, which gathered themselves together with the reunited ewe and lamb and rushed uphill in a bunch, heading towards the highest corner of the field where there was a gate to safety. Following them, he plodded up to open it, then moved far enough back for a tide of wet wool to pour through. Closing the gate, he slip-slopped back down to the water's edge and turned to strike out for the bridge – but alas, instead of finding firm ground his foot sank deeply into a sodden molehill. He sat down heavily, twisting his leg as he fell. A pain like fire shot through his ankle. He started trying to stand up, but the sound of tearing branches came from somewhere upstream and he looked round to see what it was.

End over end, turning as either its roots or its stubby branches snagged the riverbed, the tree was now lurching steadily towards him. Only then did he notice that behind it was a giant accumulation of branches, weeds and other debris followed by pent-up water and mud that was swelling the flooded valley upstream, making it twice as wide. He tried again to stand but the pain made him sink back. Using his stick, his arms and his one good leg he scrabbled desperately, dragging himself uphill. He was just in time, for with gathering speed the whole accumulation smashed into the bridge and, as if it had been made of sand rather than durable stone and mortar that had lasted almost 2,000 years, it collapsed into the maelstrom before his eyes. A huge swirling pool of water and debris swept on downriver, led by the tree, to smash through the strands of wire at the far end of the field as if they were cotton thread, a liquid rumble carrying on down the valley. Then he heard a whimper. Meg was sitting anxiously on the far bank in the lights of the Land Rover shining down from the roadside. Now *she* was marooned, with the now-uncrossable river between them. He reached for his mobile, only to remember with a jolt that he had left it lying on the kitchen table.

"Down!" he shouted urgently to his dog. "Stay!"

Chapter 2

"Holy Moley!"

Exeter meteorologist Mike Winters had just finished the umpteenth game of Patience on his mobile phone and was waking up his desk screen again in satellite imaging mode. This had just revealed the surprising monster that Lows A and B had formed. Switching to isobar charts, the tall young man was shocked to see an enormous cobweb of rings, each one closer to the other as they neared the centre, which was somewhere far out to the north east of Ireland and the dangling mulls of Scotland. As the screen refreshed itself, he could see the whole caboodle was inching to the south east and would probably tilt towards Anglesey in, what, twenty-four hours, perhaps a bit more? This did not look good. In fact, it looked like a bloody disaster in the making, so he added a loud "f*****g hell!"

His bespectacled older colleague, Caroline Cleaver, had been in doze mode, but she was now wide awake and coming over.

"Oh, Christ!" she said looking over his shoulder. "Is that real? How could that happen so quickly? It can't be."

"It is. And there's a whopper of a spring tide to add to that. Real storm surge potential, high impact stuff. I've never seen anything quite like it before. What do we do?"

It was a good question. The Met Office's 0100 shipping forecast and inshore waters forecasts had already gone out. These reports had warned of the likelihood of winds reaching gale force off Ireland, a long way short of the brewing blast he was now looking at. His immediate thought was that those in peril on the sea were in for more than an unpleasant surprise. He and Caroline had to set about sending appropriate alerts and revisions. Even when the BBC put these out at around 5.30am, they would not give everyone at sea time to run for port. The pair started on the business straight away. As they did so, there were other thoughts in Winters' mind – in particular the Michael Fish debacle. Back in October 1987 the dapper, mild bespectacled Fish, a TV weather forecast presenter, had assured viewers in Britain that although people had been ringing up about rumours of an approaching hurricane, there was no likelihood of such a phenomenon occurring in Britain.

How wrong he was. The worst hurricane-force storm in living memory followed, causing 18 deaths and smashing or uprooting thousands of trees, while the property damage bill soared to millions of pounds. Meteorologists had had egg on their face big time. If this particular monster struck land later today, or perhaps early tomorrow, wouldn't they be looking at a very similar scenario? Perhaps even something far worse?

He started to check the reports from automatic stations but was interrupted by a call. It was Peter Riorden at Met Eireann, the Met's 'sister' weather station in Dublin.

"Well hello Exeter," Riorden began. "And who do I have the pleasure of speaking to this fine morning? Young Michael Winter, I'm guessing."

Winter laughed, but he guessed the reason for the call was far from a laughing matter.

"Hello Peter. Looks like we've got a bit of a storm brewing out your way. It's just taken us by surprise."

"Ah, yes. That's Miranda."

"So, you've already named her. Damn – I was hoping we might have the pleasure."

"Oh yes, there's no flies on us. She's a bit of a brute, eh? Real romper."

The naming of storms was a task shared by both the British and Irish forecasting organisations, a 'storm' being any weather system heading their way that might warrant a 'be prepared' amber warning or a red 'take action'. 'Miranda' would have come from a jointly agreed names list for the year canvassed from the public.

"We're putting out 'red' warnings now and you'll want to do the same for sure. By the way, 'Miranda' is a particularly apt name," Riorden continued.

"How so?"

"Well, for a start she has been re-born. She had a listing back in the 2017-18 season but never got used – not enough storms! She might even have been used on later occasions if our 'Winking Weatherman' Gerald Fleming hadn't suggested 'Miranda' was a bit hackneyed."

"Hackneyed? Why?"

"Wake up my boy – Miranda was the daughter of Prospero, marooned on an island in the world's most famous storm play, *The Tempest*."

Winter laughed. "Can't see anything hackneyed in that. Nor can you, by the look of it. Why 'Winking Weatherman' by the way?"

"He was our main TV weatherman then. Always signed off with a cheeky wink. But look, there's nothing at all funny about Miranda. We've all got to batten down the hatches. I guess Connor's not there with you yet?"

Winter covered his phone mouthpiece, looked over his shoulder and said: "Car – can you call Mervyn Connor? He needs to be in on all this. Don't wake the boss until we've spoken to him though – she needs her beauty sleep."

While Caroline did this, Winters and Riorden made a rough plot of Miranda's trajectory before a final 'Let's hold on to our hats!' from the Irishman ended their call.

'The boss' Mike Winters referred to was chief exec Marion Cooper, although some of the near-2,000 Met Office staff were quite likely to refer to her behind her back as 'Miss Mastermind'. They were all rather proud of the way she had once come close to winning the TV general knowledge quiz – specialist subject the writings of Sir Walter Scott – and how she had fought to reach the position of overall IC at the Met Office.

Mervyn Connor, no underling himself, was the monitoring and forecasting wing's line manager, the kingpin they needed to take any big decisions. Cleaver was talking to him now. Winters could hear urgency in her normally calm voice.

A storm surge, particularly one as menacingly big as this one appeared to be, needed big decisions. If it looked necessary to assemble the full flood-forecasting liaison team the Met Office shared with the Environment Agency and Natural Resources Wales to raise the alarm, Connor – fairly recent widower, with a daughter at Uni in Norwich – was was the man to call it. And boy did it look necessary. He was also one of the best PR men the Met Office had, and if things looked as bad and as fast moving as this situation was likely to be, those skills would be more widely needed.

***

In the lower Wye Valley, journalist John Carter lay in bed, with rain drumming on the roof. It had been pouring with hardly a break for days.

"John?"

A small voice. He knew Phyllis was awake, just as he knew something big was on her mind – had been for some time in fact. Was she on the brink of a declaration that love was dead? They both knew that. An admission she had another lover, a rival? In one sense that would be a relief. Maybe she had spent all their money? What money, hah! Nevertheless, perhaps there was something trying to come out. She half rolled towards him. He feigned drowsiness.

"Phyll?"

There was a pause, during which he felt like a priest waiting for someone to launch into confession. But his wife baulked the moment it was on her lips. Practically fled the church in fact, not even offering a lesser sin.

"Oh, doesn't matter. It's nothing. Nothing at all."

She turned away again.

Lying with his eyes wide open, Carter imagined the slick water running off the house's glistening black slates. Out in the dark an animal gave a sharp yelp; probably a randy dog fox. Well, they were right on the edge of the forest. It was a common enough call. His mind wandered to the area where sleep is practically impossible, and thoughts of tomorrow and work loom largest of all. It was two days after press day; another weekly miracle had been brought out. But what the blithering bollocks was he going to lead the next one with? The lower Severn community that The *Clarion* served was quiet at the best of times. With everyone indoors and away from mischief because the weather was so awful, it was even quieter. Perhaps somebody would crack under the pressure of confinement and there would be a murder or a juicy bit of scandal for the paper to dig into. He shut his eyes and tried to dream up some appropriate headlines, push his concerns about Phyll out of his mind.

Out of the blue he heard his mobile ring, faintly – it was in his jacket pocket on the hall pegs. He let it ring, and it quickly stopped, only to start up again in a few seconds. Damn, what was it? He checked his bedside clock – nearly five o'clock in the morning. Either it was something urgent or scammers who cared nothing about time zones phoning from abroad. But in case it was the former he'd have to go.

He crept out on tiptoe and went downstairs barefoot. The phone had stopped ringing again by the time he got there, of course, but the caller had left a message and it was a familiar number: his photographer, 'snapper' Tad Morgan, way up the Wye Valley near Ross. He dialled the message service, wondering what was up. Tad's voice was strained.

"Johno, get some checks out. We've got urgent severe flooding alerts up here and the Environment Agency wants everybody out of the way."

He called the photographer back. Tad picked up quickly.

"How bad is it?"

"Total bloody carnage and blue murder. Never seen the river so high. It's already gone into all the houses up the Lydbrook Valley under the old viaduct, and they say there's pianos floating out of cottage windows at Brockweir. Could be the big one – there's a Severn alert too and there's the biggest tide of the year expected tomorrow early, backed by what they're calling a tidal surge. Already they're calling it a megasurge – I've never heard that term before. Like I said, it's bad enough up here but it looks like you're going to cop it from all directions down there. I'm going out with the camera now to wait for some reasonable light."

"Sounds a bit of a bugger," Carter commented. "Get what you can, and I'll head for the office. Do the police know anything about it?"

"They woke me up. There's a major national flap on and they say they fully expect casualties. Look, I don't want to be alarmist, but it could be the worst tragedy we've ever experienced, the noises the cops are making."

"I see. Call the office in half an hour and let me know what's going on – I'll be there. And that tide warning – when you said high tide is 'tomorrow' morning, did you mean 'today' tomorrow, or *tomorrow* tomorrow? I'm going to try to get a special edition out, printing around lunch if that's possible."

"The latter. You've got about 24 hours before what's beginning to look like the mother of a Biblical flood. Good luck with the special – I'll file pictures on the hoof."

Chapter 3

When Owen had not come back in over two hours, Alice started to get worried. He probably hadn't meant to leave his mobile behind, but there it was, lying on the kitchen table. He was unreachable. Given that phone reception was often poor at the best of times in this part of the valley where the hills crowded in, he might have been out of reach anyway, but the fact she couldn't even *try* to call was a worry in its own right. However, she was comforted by the fact that Owen was a resourceful man who knew how to look after himself in emergencies, and he'd find a way out of most scrapes if he got into trouble. So, she decided to let another hour pass before acting.

When there was still no sign of him and it wasn't all that long until dawn, she called Billy Davies' number – he farmed about a mile higher up the valley road beyond the James' land. She wanted to know if he knew what the situation with the river was, and whether he could drop down to the field gate where Owen was sure to be parked and see if he was all right. However, the phone kept ringing and ringing. She was about to give up and get her own little VW out of the garage when Billy's teenage son, Rod, picked up.

"Da's out. It's getting real bad here and he's gone to look to our animals. Been out about an hour – the Agency called us too when the flume alarms went off. He's on the tractor. I'll call his mobile. I'm sure he would be happy to check but it might take him a bit of time to get there. But I know he will go."

"Would I be quicker in a car do you think?" she said.

"Doubt it, the road is awash in places and you'll have to go real careful. I'll phone him now."

She put her phone down quickly so that Rod could get on with that.

Owen was feeling the cold, even though he had huddled himself up on the ground to try to keep a central core of warmth. Luckily his waterproofs were holding, although from time to time there was an annoying tiny trickle running inside his collar and down his neck. The leg still hurt like fury, but the pain was lessening a little, he felt. It wouldn't hold his weight, however, even with the help of his stick.

He knew Alice would be worried by now, and that surely meant she would check up on him somehow. She had the car to get to the gate, but with the rain still falling relentlessly – increasing in intensity, even – it might take her some time to get through.

Meg was still sitting obediently to attention on the far bank, drenched, but waiting for orders and perhaps puzzled that none came. From time to time she whimpered, and Owen had to make encouraging noises above the drumming of the rain to quieten her while keeping her in her place. He did not want her attempting to cross the water, though he knew she would do so if he asked.

The level of the river had dropped back a little after the huge head of water held back by the fallen willow and its growing accumulation of debris had rumbled on down the valley, but the rapid floodwater was still well over the banks. Owen was deeply worried by that rolling mass at the front of it that had to be far down the valley by now. People needed to be warned but there was little he could do about it for the moment. It reminded him of the disastrous Lynmouth flood of 1952, when he'd been a boy – that Devon tragedy had been caused by very similar circumstances. A storm had dumped enormous amounts of water in a short time on Exmoor, where the rivers were already full to overflowing. One by one and all the way down the twin valleys of the East and West Lyn rivers bridges tumbled as the flow became greater and greater until the force of water was rolling rocks as big as houses as if they were wine bottle corks. The rivers rushed together above Lynmouth where they swept trees, houses and vehicles down the steep gorge towards the beach and the sea. Some 34 souls were lost, taken unawares, and the damage when all was finally counted was immense. He hoped to God this wasn't happening on his river, his patch. If he hadn't been so helpless, he ought at least to be alerting people – the police perhaps – to the possible danger.

"Whisht, Meg – down! Stay!" he said as she raised her nose and gave a wolf-like howl, starting to stand. Then he saw what the dog had noticed – an erratically moving beam of light, distant but coming closer down the lane, not up, as he would have expected Alice to drive. Headlights.

It crossed his mind almost at the same moment he saw the light that whoever it was might go straight past the gate, not realising his plight. And what if Alice had gone back to bed, tired of waiting for him but trusting he would be able to look after himself? Then he recognised the sound of a tractor engine, and he knew it had to be Billy Davies' machine. Nobody else would have a tractor coming from that direction. That was reassuring, for Billy or perhaps his son would be looking to see what had happened, no doubt alerted by Alice. Rescue was on the way, thank heavens.

His own vehicle was still idling in the gateway, coughing a bit from too-rich fuel, but it was unlikely to die for the tank had been full. Then he saw the raised hydraulic arms and bucket of the tractor moving along the line of the road-hedge as it approached. It slowed and braked. Meg ran off to see who it was. Then the tractor engine was cut to tick-over too, and whoever it was shut down the Land Rover and switched off its lights, leaving only the tractor lights shining towards him.

"Halloooo! Owen!"

Billy. He shouted back, as loud as he could: "Over here, other side of the water. Busted my leg or something. Can't get over anyway."

The reassuringly ample, almost square figure of Billy, bare-headed but well wrapped in a shiny black waterproof tied at the waist with baler-twine, sploshed down the sodden field, Meg at his heels, until the two men could see each other properly through the rain. It didn't take the newcomer long to assess the situation. Only the stubs of the bridge abutments remained on each side, part underwater. Down the middle, the angry chocolate-brown water gushed relentlessly, far too deep and fast to think of wading.

"Might be able to bring the tractor down and drop the hydraulic bucket your side if you can roll near the bridge end," Billy shouted over the roar of the flood. "Can you do it? Then you can haul yourself into the bucket, see, and hold on tight."

It was practically the only solution under the circumstances. There was no other help anywhere near. Even a helicopter would be unable to operate in these conditions.

"Reckon I can," Owen said through gritted teeth, steeling himself to bear the pain as he started to roll over and over towards the seething water, "wish I was cwtched up in bed though."

Meg stood guard, whimpering, on the far bank while Billy went splosh, splosh, splosh up the field. Within a few moments the tractor started downwards in lowest gear to avoid getting into the sort of wheel-lock skid that would dump it and Billy in the flood. Its hydraulic arms and the bucket were raised aloft, as if in prayer. As he got near what was left of the bridge Billy started to drop and extend the arms. When he was as close as he dared the bucket only just reached the far side, where he set it down gently. It was impossible to speak over the noise of the water and the tractor combined, so Billy watched the black bundle of his fellow-farmer rolling towards the bucket and, finally, heaving itself inside. Moments later a hand was raised over the near edge with a thumbs-up sign.

"Well done, Boyo," Billy said to himself, lifting the bucket and backing his tractor gently away from the torrent. He could hardly draw a breath until the cargo was safely back, but then he shouted up in the hope he could be heard: "Hang tight while I get us up to the gate."

Meg knew well enough to cast wide of moving machinery as Billy gunned the tractor up the slope, its wheels spinning and throwing great clods of sodden turf behind. When they got to the top Billy lowered the bucket and the dog rushed up to lick her master's mud-caked face.

Billy drove the injured man back home in the Land Rover, then borrowed it to drive to his own home to get his son's help to retrieve the tractor.

After Owen had called the police and the Environment Agency to warn anyone downstream of a possible disaster in the making, if it hadn't already happened, Alice immediately drew a bath for him to soak in then helped him towel his black hair and matted chest.

"Come along my gorilla-man," she said using her favourite pet name for him, "Here, get into these pyjamas."

She tucked him up in bed with a hot drink, no 'ifs' or 'buts'. She called Meg in from the dog's nest in the hay, rubbed her down properly and treated her to a bowl of bread in warm milk in front of the Aga. Quite soon man and dog were both asleep and snoring loudly. Alice hoped Owen's leg, which was red and swollen from the top of the calf down to his toes, was nothing more than a bad sprain. She could feel no breaks, but when they were able to they would have to have this properly checked.

In the early light of day, she could see through the still-pouring rain down into the bottom of the valley. She had looked at it in many spells of bad weather before, but it was never like this. The river was now a vast elongated lake that had swallowed smaller fields and half of the bigger ones, and any stock had crowded back onto the drier land. Only the tops of the taller trees above the water marked the snaky line of the original river course. Most of the pollarded bankside willows were completely under. Down the middle of the lake ran a swirling current of muddy wind-streaked water full of debris ripped from its path and carried along. Then her heart missed a beat – a white blob, a sheep, clearly dead, was moving with the flow, rolling over and over. Nothing to be done for that one, then – but she hoped their own stock was well away from the same fate. Then she was overcome with a feeling of helplessness. There was nothing, absolutely nothing she thought she could do to help anyone or anything except themselves in these circumstances.

She poured herself another cup of tea from the big teapot and then tried to telephone Billy's wife, Pru, but the line was dead. As was often the case in bad storms, the wires were probably down.

Chapter 4

In Met Office HQ in Exeter, staff were desperately trying to estimate the true potential of the storm. By now it had become quite clear they were in disaster territory far exceeding the worst of so-called 'Storm of the Century' Ciara in relatively recent 2020. Some day workers were appearing early after being called in early as a matter of extreme urgency. There was much shaking of rain off hats, coats and umbrellas.

Mervyn Connor had been woken out of his dreams and he'd arrived with his curly red hair and just-grown beard tousled after a well-over-the-speed-limit drive from his Tavistock home. With his key players Connor had taken out the Environment Agency's hard copy flood risk area charts and they had them spread on the floor, trying to match them together into one big Wales and West map. From time to time the Scot rubbed his forehead or tugged at his beard. "I'm buggered!" was the only comment he had passed on the situation so far.

"And when's our highest tide?" he shot at Caroline Cleaver. His blue eyes were still bleary.

"About this time tomorrow morning – not *this* morning, I mean. But not far away."

"I'm buggered!" Connor said again, then, "What's the latest rain situation?"

Not good, Mike Weaver told him, not good at all. The outer edge of Miranda, the huge mass of tightly packed isobars heading their way, was toying with the rain front that for days had stretched between Snowdonia and Dartmoor and was feeding it with a steady stream of even more heavily moisture-laden Atlantic air. Neither the jet stream, now edging to the north of this threatening pattern, nor the big high-pressure cell to the south, were going anywhere quickly. It was all destined to stay on track: the now-malevolent Miranda and her megasurge was going to ram into them at about the peak of high tide. And it was going to go on raining and raining, and then some. With the ground already soaked and the rivers full to bursting, indeed over their banks in many places, things looked bad.

"*Really?* A monster tidal surge *and* overflowing rivers? Really? Bugger me!"

Cleaver caught Winter's eye and grinned at him, unnoticed she hoped, over Connor's head. As she did so she was aware of other people gathering behind them, trying to get a look at what was going on.

"Right," Connor said, suddenly standing up straight. "Let's get things started. We'll need to get all these areas cleared, people certainly and stock if we can. Any vessels, especially small fishing boats, must come in as fast as possible. If they can't make port, they should prepare to ride out something nasty. This looks like the big one we never wanted to happen. Mike, you get on to police, TV and radio. Press after that. Caroline, liaise with the Environment Agency please. I need to get my Minister out of his cosy bed. This means a Cobra meeting, that's for sure. I'll buzz Miss Mastermind now and tell her what's going on."

The calls did not take long. He left to take a quick shower and then catch a hastily chartered helicopter to London, flight time just over an hour. A car was being arranged to whisk him from London City Airport to Westminster.

***

Around the swampy lagoons in the Magor wildlife reserve down on the Severn-side Gwent Levels, and across the flat lands of the river's east bank between the Cotswold scarp and the river, criss-crossed by a network of drainage channels locally known as 'reans' on both sides of the river, a remarkable migration was underway at dawn. Local people afoot at first light were astonished to see amazing numbers of frogs on the move, all apparently quitting their watery habitats and heading towards high ground. The same sort of thing was happening further south, across the Somerset Levels, and indeed over a great deal of the low-lying areas of coastland in Wales and the Westcountry. Milk float drivers, postmen and early commuters alike had to take pains to avoid them on the roads. Occasionally amphibians even flopped into houses if the doors were left open, all single-mindedly and blindly heading in the same direction.

Dwellers in these places who did not yet know of Miranda's approach might have noticed that a large number of police cars were about on the roads, and if they had turned on their radios, TVs and mobiles they would have learned that people living in flood-vulnerable areas were being warned to be prepared to evacuate and told to keep listening for further information. They were also being told that several schools might close and they should check if this was the case locally before sending their children in.

What they weren't being told just yet, for fear of spreading perhaps unnecessary alarm, was that the situation was beginning to look far, far worse than was being let on. Behind the scenes the police had already started gently evacuating those Westcountry households deemed most at risk, and some schools on higher ground were being prepared as evacuation centres.

***

At 9.15 am in Cabinet Office Briefing Room A (contracted to a more usable 'Cobra'), 70 Whitehall, terse-voiced Environment Minister Peter Grove told the many people still assembling round the long table that the urgently-arranged helicopter bringing Met Office information chief Mervyn Connor up from Exeter had landed and he would be with them shortly at pretty much the same time the Prime Minster would also make an entrance. She would be wanting a comprehensive – and reassuring – statement to read to the nation at around 1pm that day. Coffee had been sent for.

The small and neatly-dressed Grove played back to the 15 people already present a recording of a telephone briefing he'd just had with the Chief Constable of Avon and Somerset police, who reported that her HQ at Portishead, just outside Bristol, had been hastily set up as the coordination centre for "Operation Sandbag".

What they didn't hear was his opening overtures with the policewoman. No, he'd had to impress on her, he was not over-exaggerating. This could potentially be one of the biggest disasters Britain had ever had to face in peacetime. Eventually she had got the message, but he realised it might be just as hard to get everyone present to realise the weight of the situation that was now developing.

"Operation Sandbag – what sort of a name is that?" asked Angela Peters, Green MP for Brighton and one of a handful of coastal-area MPs who had been brought in, some reluctantly. "What exactly are we looking at?"

"Well, I suggest you take this in, all of you," said Grove, "Storm Miranda is going to hit us with a massive tidal surge. Hence this Cobra meeting. Widespread damage and probably many fatalities are predicted."

"Last time we had a tidal surge alert it didn't amount to much," Peters said, pouting her lower lip and looking around at the faces at the table for affirmation.

"I don't think we're going to be so lucky this time by all accounts," Grove said grimly, giving his interrupter a glare. He indicated with a nod towards the door that Connor had just been shown into the room. "Ah, here's our man. Once the PM is here, we can get started. I'll now hand proceedings over to the Home Secretary, who will be our chair. The briefing papers are coming round now."

And indeed they were, delivered at speed by an aide around the green-topped table.

After showing Connor to a seat, Grove went to the young but already steel-grey haired Gordon Wright, bent and whispered in his ear before settling into the empty seat behind the chairman. "It's all yours now, Home Secretary. I hope it doesn't take as long as bloody Brexit – if anybody starts to get windy, chop them off with a broadside. Apparently, we don't have much time to get moving, especially the Army and Police." He glanced across the table at the uniformed General Sir Denis Hawling, who was sitting between Michael Saunders from the Environment Agency and the Chief Commissioner of the Met.

At that moment there was a scraping of chairs as the whole assembly, apart from Connor, who did not know the protocol, stood up when the youthful British Prime Minister entered. She had unbuttoned her rain-spattered coat but hadn't taken it off. Connor hurriedly stood too, and after greetings all around everyone sat, settled down, fiddled with the papers or pens, and with one accord looked towards him.

Swallowing, he stood up again and gave them all he knew. These combinations of wind and rain and tide were unprecedented, at least in modern times, so far as he could ascertain. At high tide early tomorrow morning – the largest tide of the year – a huge surge of water would slam into the southern half of the British Isles backed by a monumental blow: violent storm to hurricane force winds of 11 to 12 on the Beaufort wind-strength scale. Ireland, of course, had already seen the danger and was preparing its west and south-west coastal communities for the worst, while in England and Wales the worst of the surge would run at the land from both the Irish Sea and the Western approaches…"

"What's the height of the wave we're looking at?" somebody interrupted without going through the Chair.

"Not so much a wave, you have to understand, but a *surge*," he responded, hoping there wouldn't be a lot of interruptions like this to waste more time. "That means a big, big rise in water levels over a sustained period. In fact, it will rise and go on rising, and once it hits the land it will be pressed by not just the water behind it, but by the force of the wind. Anywhere low-lying is at considerable risk, and the places it makes landfall particularly so…"

"But what *height* of wave?" the questioner persisted, and Connor could see he was struggling with the 'surge' concept. Better perhaps give him and any others like him something to visualise even if it meant scaring the wits out of them.

"We're looking at 15, even 20 feet of extra water," he said. "It's impossible to be more precise. And I'm afraid that's on top of 'normal' high tide levels which, remember, are already the biggest of the year. But I'm also afraid that isn't all."

"Well, *what* else is there, Mr Connor?" the Home Secretary prompted. Connor swallowed a glass of water and took a deep breath – he had to give impact to what followed.

"Well this … practically the whole country is saturated by two weeks of unbroken heavy rain – rain that won't be stopping anytime soon – and most rivers can't take any more. In tidal river reaches and for unknowable distances above we have absolutely no predictions for what happens when a surge of this size meets major floodwater coming downriver. Places like the Severn Estuary are particularly at risk, and there are already signs of an especially worrying flooding incident developing on the River Teme which flows into that system. It looks as if there will have to be mass evacuation of many areas of the whole Severn basin below Worcester all the way down to South Wales, and some in Somerset and North Devon on the opposite bank. Some relocation of people is already underway. And there must be urgent action on flood-prevention measures like sandbagging – again underway hopefully. But we're late on the ball with this and we won't be able to protect everybody or everything. Property and stock will certainly be lost. And people, too, I'm very much afraid."

General Hawling, who had so far been attentive but silent, cleared his throat loudly at this and got a nod from the Home Secretary in the chair to proceed. He stood up, while Connor, still standing, fell silent.

"I'd like to back up Mr Connor on this point. I hope everybody realises how serious this is. We have just started up one of the largest mobilisations in modern times. Our trucks and other vehicles, including landing craft and amphibious vehicles are heading for all especially vulnerable areas plus the manpower to give whatever assistance is necessary. The Air Force and Navy are at this moment deploying reconnaissance and rescue craft and liaising with us and the other government agencies through the police HQ at Bristol. Every man – or woman – who hasn't got a role is currently filling sandbags as fast as they are able."

He earned a wry smile from many for the last point. And then he turned to the Prime Minister.

"I apologise, Prime Minister, for acting without say-so from you or this committee, but we had to take appropriate action as soon as we could. I hope you are able to approve Ma'am?"

"Quite so."

Sir Denis sat down. With a nod to him, Connor continued: "There are predictive maps in your briefing papers of the likely extent of floodwater and I would like you all to study them carefully to see how they might affect the areas or organisations you represent. Because of the sudden turn of events there are still things that need urgent attention, for example making halls and schools available as evacuation centres. And people might have to be billeted in ordinary households until we are sure the emergency is over. I need not remind anyone that there is a big security risk for evacuated properties, and the police I understand are deploying as best they can to attend to this..."

He got grunted accord from the police contingent.

"And very importantly, we have to look very carefully at our power and water facilities to make sure they are as flood-proof as they can be. Power cuts are a big possibility, especially if the grid must be shut down over safety concerns. And let's not forget we have nuclear power plants in vulnerable areas – Dungeness, Hartlepool, Heysham 1 and 2, Hinkley Point, Hunterston B, Torness and Sizewell B. Of these Hinkley Point, on the Severn Estuary, seems the most at risk, although the former N-stations higher up the Severn at Berkeley and Oldbury are being dismantled and still hold radioactive material. Special attention is being given to these areas as I speak, I believe."

A loud "Ahem!" came from the Prime Minister and in the silence that followed she looked at the speaker and said, "Mr Connor, can you tell us if this is a Westcountry-specific problem? Are there implications for the rest of the country – London for example?"

Aware of the London-centric nature and concerns of the current government, Connor knew he had to make specific assurances on this issue, but he also needed to represent the situation for the rest of Britain as well. It was time to revisit the disastrous North Sea Flood of 1953. Apart from anything else it would concentrate minds on the real threats a big storm-surge posed.

"In this instance the focus of Miranda will be on the westward side of the British Isles but, yes, practically every coastal region will be affected in some way. Many of us around this table are probably not aware of the North Sea Flood of 1953, which was particularly deadly for the south-east of Britain as well as the coasts of Denmark and the Netherlands – 307 people were killed on land and over 200 at sea in Britain alone, and many thousands were left homeless here and in Europe. You ask about London. Well, yes, there was widespread flooding in '53. It was one of the reasons the Thames Barrage was built, and on that score, nobody should be complacent about the safety that it gives the capital.

"However, because Miranda's surge is on the other side of Britain – and because of the barrage – I don't expect London to be quite so challenged as it was in 1953, but I wouldn't want to be definite about that because it's quite hard to predict something you've never experienced before. I'm afraid there will be local coastal flooding almost everywhere, some severe to very severe, and precautions should be taken now, evacuations if necessary. However, the West is facing the most extreme danger this time."

He paused and asked for more water, sipped and then concluded: "Raise any particular concerns you have as well as requests for clarification. I see from the briefing papers you have the telephone numbers and email addresses of all the agencies involved in Operation Sandbag as well as the principal players. Now I'm going to hand you back to the Chair, who will, I understand, tell you of all the special powers this committee can invoke. Home Secretary."

Home Secretary Wright exchanged a glance with the Prime Minister then, without standing, thanked Connor and Sir Denis.

"Right," he said with a business-like air but a deeply worried face, "Let's get started shall we. Any questions?"

***

Another helicopter lift, this time to the Portishead Police HQ, was being arranged for Connor, Michael Saunders of the Environment Agency and three of the other delegates. While he waited in an anteroom for the flight call, he and Saunders were given the immediate job of getting together a brief statement for the media. The word was getting around and questions were already starting to trickle in about what was up.

Sandy-haired Saunders was an old friend and they had worked together on a few flood protection projects. The

Environment Agency was responsible for Britain's sea and river flood defences and there were often occasions when accurate weather projections were needed so that the Agency knew how high and how strong their barriers needed to be. Saunders looked concerned and, once they were alone together, he told Connor of his fears.

"We're simply not up to something this big," he said. "Hardly anything in the Westcountry will be able to stand up to it. Same old problem, there's not enough cash to make things properly safe. You can tell them that until you're blue in the face but unless something smacks them on the nose, they shrug it all off. Well, they're going to get smacked this time!"

Connor laughed. "That's for sure," he said. "The trouble is, when things go this wrong, they start looking around for someone to blame. Guess who's in the firing line?"

Another laugh from Connor. "Me too," he said wryly.

Connor fielded a couple of calls while they worked on the press release but felt ill-prepared to include any technical or strategic information other than that people should tune into their local TV and radio stations for updates from the police and emergency services, and if they thought they were in any danger they should act, and move fast. The situation was far too fluid to call what was going to happen, or even to predict a timeframe. There was one last incoming telephone call as he posted the release online, where it would be widely distributed to all outlets – and even as he answered it, somebody was beckoning them at the door to hurry for the flight.

"Can we say Storm Miranda is anything to do with global warming?" the BBC wanted to know.

"Sorry, we're too busy making emergency provisions to look into anything like that," was his reply. "That's for the inquest to decide."

Chapter 5

In his rain-rattled corrugated iron-shod utility building offices on the SevernSide Business Park, John Carter started laying out a *Clarion* special edition. When he had left his house earlier, Phyllis was either still asleep or pretending to be so. He'd had to navigate the company Fiesta through river-sized running puddles on the steep downhill road and across town to the industrial units, and because the precipitation was relentless, he'd parked at the slightly higher ground behind a parade of shops. It meant he didn't have to splosh through anything much walking to the office, although his untidy blond hair was quickly soaked and slicked flat when he'd made a dash for it.

He had decided on a wrap-round for his flood special edition plus a complete new centre spread, which had meant ripping out a collection of pictures of local notables at various presentations. No great loss, that. Using the collection of excellent pictures Tad Morgan had already filed, the back, inside back and middle pages were already coming together quite quickly.

The mechanics of a wrap-round are simple: the current week's 'old' paper loses its original front and back and inside-front and inside-back contents, plus the spread, for new pages, then the whole shebang is reconstructed on-screen and fired electronically down the road to the printer – in the *Clarion*'s case, in Newport. As a 'free' newspaper a special did not ostensibly make any money. However, since the rival publication, a daily up in Gloucester, had gone weekly, suffering the same rapid decline as many regional papers, Carter could steal a march on them. And by adding the specials he gave out to his own week's distribution figure, he could bump up the overall circulation by a considerable amount. A higher circulation usually attracted more advertising revenue in the long run. But occasions for specials were rare as hens' teeth: Carter had to put their journalistic worth ahead of any commercial concerns.

One of Carter's first tasks had been to check that the printers could handle extra work and they'd told him 'yes' provided he could fire the pages over by 12.30. He'd also had to get an OK from his boss, the line manager somewhere in deepest Surrey who was forever muttering about 'yield' – profit left after the expense of bringing the publication out. Even if the boss did care more about revenue than the news that was printed in his nationwide chain, he had fortunately turned his radio on early that morning and heard some already-alarming news about a possible flood. Carter got his blessing for an extra "10,000 – max". Practically all he had to do now was write a heading and a little piece of background for the inside front with 'turn to' under the heading. And he asked the ad-girls to phone round newsagents to put out placards with "FLOOD ALERT SPECIAL" on them, and to expect papers by early afternoon.

Then somebody rang about frogs.

"Umn all over the place up yere – frawgs everywhere," the caller said in a thick local accent. "You orta come'n get a picture. Big 'uns, little 'uns, everywhere. Shall I send you summat from my phone?"

"Ok," Carter said distractedly. He was anxious to get on with his task. "Where are you calling from, by the way?"

Somewhere up in the outback, was the answer. For future editions Carter needed different viewpoints as the flood developed, so he asked the man if he'd mind contributing a few words and pictures in a day or so. He took the number, and told the caller how to transmit pictures in, anything flood-related including the 'frawgs'.

Back to the job in hand. Now, when was the last big flood in this area? He had an idea it might have been 2007, something like that. He'd been living and working in Gloucester at that time and things had been grim for a while. He tapped "Severn floods" into his computer's search engine, notebook at the ready to jot down anything in the way of parallels.

Helen, one of the three girls on the ad-desks brought him a cup of coffee and a shortbread biscuit.

"There you go Johnny – you look busy," she said. "What's up? Apart from the rain, that is?"

He told her as much as he knew and asked her if she knew anyone in low-lying areas who might be at risk. Carter wasn't quite sure if he managed to convey the full extent and seriousness of the threat.

"I've got an auntie in Brockweir," she said. "I'll give her a call later."

It wasn't hard to locate information about flooding in 2007, and from his own memory he could fill in a great deal of detail. He was about to close down on his research and get the thing written when something else in the Googled listings caught his eye: "*Severn Flood Disaster, 1607*".

Now that did look interesting. He opened the item more out of curiosity than anything else – after all, what bearing would something from the seventeenth century have on modern Britain?

What he saw snapped him wide awake and he had to read on ...

The most striking item on the Wikipedia page was a contemporary drawing of a church in water up to the edge of the nave roof. It also showed a deep, unending lake as far as the horizon, with people in the foreground either clinging to roofs or to the tops of near-submerged trees, or floundering and waving up to their necks in the flood, along with their cattle, sheep, horses and goats all treading water, all in imminent danger of drowning.

Carter read the picture caption: *"The church is thought to be St Mary's at Nash, near Newport,"* and he moved on rapidly to *"The disastrous events of 1607…*

"On January 30, around noon, the coasts of the Bristol Channel suffered from unexpectedly high flooding that broke the coastal defences in several places. Low-lying places in Devon, Somerset, Gloucestershire and South Wales were inundated.

"The devastation was particularly severe on the Welsh side, extending from Laugharne in Carmarthenshire to above Chepstow in Monmouthshire. Cardiff was the most badly affected town."

Carter thought, "That's a big part of my patch." He had to read the next paragraph twice, because its contents were particularly hard to swallow.

"It is estimated that 2,000 or more people were drowned, houses and villages were swept away, an estimated 200 square miles of farmland were inundated, and livestock destroyed, wrecking the local economy along the coasts of the Bristol Channel and Severn Estuary."

This was not a part of British history that Carter had been told about in his school textbooks – 2,000 drownings, stock and farming wiped out over a huge area of the country, the sea encroaching as far as Glastonbury Tor in Somerset on one side of the Bristol Channel and lapping around the homes of Wales' premier city on the other.

History books do have to be selective and the nation – then as now London-centric – had other preoccupations that recorders presumably deemed more worthy at the time. King James was on the throne and Guy Fawkes and his fellow conspirators had made an unsuccessful attempt to blow up parliament, the Holy Bible was being translated into English for the first time, and William Shakespeare was among the actors in a London theatre group The King's Men. In 1607, he hadn't yet written *The Tempest*, one of his most famous plays (c.1611), although as a frequent traveller between London and Stratford-on-Avon he almost certainly witnessed some flooding if the water backed-up on his local river. Did this perhaps spark the idea for his storm-driven drama?

Carter quickly trawled the internet further, nervously aware time was running short and he would soon have to send his pages off. Most accounts he found told of the rivers and sea rising quickly, then continuing to rise, as the Severn Bore does on incoming tides today. Unwary spectators are often caught out by the still-growing surge behind the leading crest of the bore and get an unexpected soaking.

For the main part the whole disastrous incident of 1607 was attributed to a storm surge, an unusually high tide pushed on by extreme weather arriving from the west. But here and there he found references to another possible force at work. Was it a tsunami, some commentators asked?

The tsunami idea was not infeasible. The trigger for such a phenomenon could be seismic activity in the Irish Sea or further west, along the ridge of huge submerged mountains running north-south along the middle of the Atlantic. Some internet accounts did point to an earthquake being recorded in the Westcountry at around that time, although others stated there was indeed a series of tremors but put the date much later in the year than the flood.

Carter felt he now had enough background to compile his story and was about to shut down the computer when another item caught his eye – "*The 1607 Flood – What Did the Frogs Know?*"

He could not afford to give the item any more than a short look-over. Some 1607 reports told of local people noticing 'plagues' of frogs prior to the flood. Curious. He cut and saved the contemporary pamphlet that also contained a lengthy rant against the rife sin and lawlessness of the times. It was titled *"God's warning to the people of England by the great overflowing of the waters or floods"*.

Once Carter had put his piece together and placed a cracking picture from Tad of a man and woman each paddling rustic coracles up the main street of Lower Lydbrook, he was left with the choice of two possible splash headings. One was

URGENT FLOOD
ALERT

and the other was

TSUNAMI
ALERT

Erring on caution (but sorely tempted by the more emotive word) he chose 'Flood' over 'Tsunami'.

Only when the pages were safely off did it cross his mind that he ought to be going back home. But home to what?

Chapter 6

When normally unflappable John Wiltshire at the Environment Agency's Tewkesbury outpost had put the phone down after an agitated call from farmer Owen James, he knew he had to hit the panic button. Clearly a major incident was in the offing. No, not just 'major' but 'major major'.

On his desktop computer he called up the flood risk map of the Teme watershed. Somewhere up in the hillside headwaters to the south of Newtown and below Owen James' land, a growing pent-up mass of water and debris was rolling relentlessly downstream and obliterating most of the things in its path. It would soon encounter vital road bridges and waterside homes and settlements.

This early morning the Teme was already racing bank-high because of the incessant rain and had already gone over in a few places. It was a far cry from summers of late when the tortuously winding 80-mile-long river had sometimes dried to a feeble trickle, abstraction being blamed for the demise. Once the latest mass of water that Owen James had reported joined it, the watercourse would be a very dangerous beast indeed, thundering along at, what, five or six miles an hour, all the way down to its confluence with the River Severn at Worcester. And he knew the Severn itself was already well up

– alerts had started more than a day ago for that river's floodwater peak approaching Worcester round about now.

As he made all the necessary emergency calls to alert and protect his patch, he saw in his mind's eye the lower towns of the Severn Vale, Upton, Tewkesbury, Gloucester, waking to what looked like one of the biggest flooding threats in his lifetime – and he soon learned that wasn't all. When he telephoned his boss at the Agency's HQ in Bristol he learned the man had just been helicoptered urgently to London for a Cobra Committee meeting. On the committee agenda: an imminent and serious storm surge in the Bristol Channel. A huge floodwater peak was coming downriver, an unprecedentedly high, power-driven tide would be going up in the other direction. The old conundrum of what would happen if an irresistible force met an immovable object came to mind. It was without a shadow of a doubt a perfect storm in the making.

Operation Sandbag was starting to get into full swing when Connor and Saunders flew back to the Portishead HQ from the Cobra meeting in a bucking helicopter, landing bumpily on the sports field in front of a pavilion. The other passengers were Sir Denis Hawling and two area MPs. On his way Connor felt the need for widespread and decisive action was gaining more urgency with every passing minute. A guide had been sent to take them along a treelined avenue, with their heads bent against the driving wind and rain, to the operations room.

Thankfully the police taskforce had already managed to paste together a large table-top contour Ordnance Survey map of the entire area, from the tip of Land's End all the way up to North Wales, across a swathe of the West Midlands including the Warwickshire Avon Valley in the east and over to the extreme west of the Principality.

The Chief Constable, Dr Christine Lees, short haired, bespectacled and small-boned but tough, introduced herself. Somebody took the MPs off for breakfast in the canteen while the rest of the party surveyed the map. As yet at-risk areas had not been fully marked but a cartographer was directing where these should be drawn. Even as the newcomers took the situation in, somebody stepped forward and hatched-in an area to the west of Worcester on the map's plastic cover, then marked another broad area straddling the River Severn from Shrewsbury down to Worcester.

"What are those?" asked Connor, tugging his beard.

"I can tell you all about those," said Saunders at his elbow. "They show flood water moving down the River Severn and the River Teme. I suppose you could call a lot of this 'normal' stuff at the best of times, because the lighter-shaded areas are on our permanent flood-risk maps – they are expected to go under every ten years or so. We issue them to anyone living in these areas and you can call them up on the internet if you need to. But as you can see, there is a darker outline here on the Severn near Shrewsbury, and on the upper Teme, where we have something of a situation developing at this moment. In fact, we will be updated by our men on the ground as things develop. It isn't looking good."

"Situation? Develop?"

Saunders had a quiet voice, but one that carried authority and demanded people's attention, and he was good at explaining things. He relayed what John Wiltshire had reported about all the remote flow meters in the Teme headwaters going off scale in the night, and the special worry about a huge mass of water and debris moving downstream from Owen James' land that was just now surging into the main River Teme. It was, by all accounts, a 'bit of a worry' and in his mind it posed a threat not only to riverside householders and farms, but also to the major bridges of the area – not a few of them ancient monuments.

"And these are expected to, what, dissipate over the floodplains? Isn't that what they usually do?"

But Saunders was already shaking his head. "No – I'm afraid not, not this time anyway," he said. "We've already got standing water saturation on all the floodplain areas. The extra

Severn water I'm expecting will work its way downstream in an extreme but predictable way, but the Teme – well, I'm not so sure about the Teme. When it gets to the lower part of the river, I would expect it to accelerate rather than anything, and it will still carry a considerable burden – uprooted trees, bits of buildings, drowned animals, even vehicles. Who knows?"

"And it will eventually reach the Severn – when? Where?

"At Worcester. Some time later today."

"And then?"

A shrug. "As far as I can see – and my main man in the area agrees with me – all the lower Severn towns are in imminent danger at round about the same time as the storm surge is ploughing upstream – a situation we've never ever known before and certainly not one we've ever planned for."

"Je..!" Connor started, but turned the words that had come to mind into a cough instead. "We can do without that. Is everyone aware, by the way, that we're looking at strong winds too. They'll be getting up just about now, setting in from the south west, veering west later and reaching severe gale force, probably hurricane strength in gusts. That should last at least until lunchtime tomorrow, or longer if the system stalls on its way over. That's the added factor exacerbating this problem."

The Chief Constable was nodding. "We're shutting down both Severn bridges early this afternoon – all vehicles, not just lorries. And it's not just for their safety – we need to keep the carriageways clear for emergency vehicles. There are bulletins going out now on radios and TV asking people not to make any car journeys that aren't essential. Lorries will have to go back or park op. They can't even take the long way round to South Wales through Gloucester, because that's in one of the big risk areas with some dodgy causeways around the town and expected flooding along the A40 and A48 even without the current situation. The Cardiff-Gloucester rail line won't allow trains through as the water rises, and because of the wind gusts airlines have been advised to put flights on hold until the danger is past. As you can probably see Cardiff, Bristol and Birmingham airports are the most likely to be badly affected, but the alert covers London airports and the Midlands.

"Better safe than sorry is our message. We've done our best to reach everyone but of course we can't be sure. We've asked them to make sure anything loose and dangerous like roofing sheets are tied or weighted down. Farmers we hope are moving vulnerable stock to high ground.

"We've also asked for help to identify anyone at risk who might not see or hear our messages. I've cancelled leave here and all our phones are waiting for call-ins. Mobile units are out spreading the word and we've identified evacuation centres. The Army is sandbagging wherever it can and of course they're on standby for rescues and evacuations – thanks Sir Denis," she acknowledged with a wag of her head in his direction. "We've done what we can, I think, but I do hope it's enough…"

Here Christine Lees paused – somebody had passed her a newspaper, and she took a moment to glance at it. Then she held it up by its corners so that everyone could see the *Clarion* special front page splash,

URGENT
FLOOD
ALERT

"As you can see," she said, "freshly printed from across the Severn Bridge, the word's getting around. Somebody's on the ball!"

She paused to take a sip from a glass of water, then looked around the assembled task force.

"Now, Mr Connor, and you, Mr Saunders, it's up to you to help us predict what's likely to happen."

Chapter 7

John Carter paused outside his front door. There didn't seem to be any sign of life within – no lights, no noise of any kind – but when he opened the door and stepped inside he thought he heard a sob.

"Phyll?" he shouted from the hallway. He put his car keys on the hall stand and started up the stairs. The bedroom door was ajar, and he pushed it further and walked in. Phyllis, dressed in jeans, a white shirt and a red cardigan top with a faux-fur-collared rain jacket over that, was lying on her back on top of an unmade bed with her hands over her face. She was sobbing. Beside her lay an opened suitcase, fully packed with some underwear beside it.

"What's up, Phyll?"

He went over and sat on the edge of the bed beside her, put a hand on her shoulder. But she shrugged it off and edged herself away.

"Don't!"

There was forbidding sharpness in the rebuke.

"Well, what are you doing?"

"I'm going home," she said with her hands still over her face. "Now."

Home – that meant Bath, or rather very near it, where her parents lived. Quite a little drive in the best of weathers.

"But what's all this about? Won't you tell me? And anyway, you can't go in this ... they've already shut the bridges and they're telling people not to take vehicles out. It's a full-scale emergency. The river's coming over at Newnham and Minsterworth so you won't be able to go that way either. Haven't you heard?"

She drew her hands away from her face, looked at the ceiling rather than at him, her eyes red rimmed from crying.

"I can't help that. I'll go up the valley and round the back of Cinderford. And don't try to stop me."

"Phyll...you mustn't. Not now anyway. Not anytime come to that. Can't we work it out?"

But she sat up suddenly, roughly pushed the rest of her clothes into the suitcase and snapped the catches shut. She swung her long legs off the bed, stood up and picked up the case.

He moved to the door and stood in her way.

"You mustn't. I can't let you. It's not our car, anyway," he tried desperately.

But she came around the bed and walked straight at him until he had to give way. She brushed past him and he heard her footsteps rush downstairs. The front door slammed, and the car door. It started up and moved off with a squeal of tyres. Now the house really felt empty..

***

Alice James took her husband a cup of tea at lunchtime and asked if he felt able to come down for some food – a cheese omelette, perhaps? She imagined comfort food would be the most acceptable under the circumstances. He smiled at the idea, then rolled back the duvet. They both inspected the bad leg as if it was a museum exhibit.

Owen poked the red, sore bit with his forefinger. "Still hurts like hell when I move it, and it's puffy round the ankle. But I really don't think there's anything broken," he said. "Never know what to do with these things – rest it or make it do some work? I bet if you asked a roomful of doctors half of them would say one thing and half the other. If you bring up my stick, I'll see if I can get mobile."

"All right," said Alice, pulling the cover back, "You finish that tea and I'll be back in a flash. But no heroics, mind!"

He grimaced at her retreating figure – the ankle really was sore, but it was worth trying to get up. He sat up against the bedhead and finished the tea, then gingerly worked his leg round so that he could drop both feet on the floor. He achieved this manoeuvre just as he heard his wife's steps coming back up the stairs.

"Owen!" she said reprovingly when she saw him half standing.

But it was all right – or partly so, anyway. He could stand on the one good leg, but it was as yet impossible to put any weight on the poorly one. With her help he carefully drew on his trousers and by using his stick and with a little more help from her he got to the stairs, then down them and into the kitchen. Meg bounded up to nuzzle him. He sat at the kitchen table while Alice busied herself frying the promised omelette, looking down through the window at the swollen river.

"I wonder how they got on with all that water and muck going downstream?" Owen speculated. "What's it all looking like today?"

"The river's still well up," she said. "Sometimes standing here you can actually hear the roar of it."

It was swirling along angrily and over its banks. But no worse than earlier, she thought, so perhaps it had peaked. Then she noticed something.

"Owen – I don't know if you can see this, but I think the rain's slowing if you can believe it."

"Hah!" he said. "At last. There's a blessing for us all. But will it last?"

A sudden buffet of wind moments later shook the walls of the sturdily built house, accompanied by a machine gun-like rattle of hail on the windowpane, making them look at each other with dismay. It was not over yet.

***

Of all the times Colin Roach had put to sea for scallops, this current session had seemed to be the worst. Not only had the catch been meagre – the dredges bringing up more empty shells than living ones – but also 17 year old Jago Nancarrow was rolling on the floor in the fish-processing area, the sickest he had ever seen him, and his other crewman, Pete Walby, had broken a finger. And then, while they were still fishing 14 or so miles out, the storm had started to be a big problem. Now at the outer edge of their radio range, they'd heard the weather update. Already three French boats that had been shellfish dredging nearby had upped their gear and set off hastily towards France. Reluctantly, Roach hauled up his own gear and stowed it.

But after a quick calculation he reckoned he would never make it through the tricky ground close to Newlyn Harbour at low tide, let alone get in on the following rising tide if things were going to be as bad as the reports were predicting. That left him no choice but to try to ride it out short-handed in the Western Approaches, as far away from harm as he could manage.

Already it was lashing – had been since they started out in fact – and the sea had become what he called 'trech'rus', with swift currents running randomly this way and that like angry snakes. And the wind was also unpredictably wayward, skittering everywhere and throwing up streamers of foam over a long, deep swell. All the same, the heavily-built Penzance-registered *Jocasta,* a shade under 15 metres, could handle most things the sea and weather chucked at her, he reckoned. However, they might need a fair measure of luck. It was no use pretending it wasn't a dangerous situation after such dire shipping warnings. The two men and the boy were as well-tackled-up as they could be to face this with inflatable life vests over oilskins – Maritime and Coastguard Agency-approved Personal Inflation Devices with harnesses and D-rings that would make it easier for them to be fished out of the water if needed. The vessel's lifeboat – a rubber inflatable protected in a large water tank-like plastic shell – was ready to be deployed, and had a weak-link line attached to the deck which would break away if *Jocasta* sank. So they weren't entirely unprepared.

When the wind turned to blow more reliably from the west, Roach was a little happier and he put the boat about to face into it, dropped anchor on a long chain, and disengaged the Kelvin engine but kept it running. They were over a shell and sand bottom, according to the chart, so the anchor could drag a bit if – or more likely when – it got rough. The chart also showed there was nothing hazardous near their position, such as an underwater reef, unless they were pulled a very long way indeed. The latest storm forecast had given the wind veering nor-nor-west after a while, then north west, a familiar pattern with Atlantic depressions. Even with a fair amount of dragging things looked as safe as they could be.

Walby, with his broken index finger lashed to the next good middle finger with elastic plaster from the First Aid box, checked 'the lad' Nancarrow and came back to report. "Not very good," was the verdict. "Should get him up here where we can keep an eye on him. It's only motion sickness but we know how bad that feels. You just want to die."

"Wait a minute and I'll help you move him," said Roach. "I'd better see if I can call Newlyn and tell them we're staying out. Give a position. Don't want them to forget all about us."

The VHF reception was worse now, but he got through, gave their coordinates and told Harry Cook on the receiving end they were still hoping to weather it out.

"Good luck with that," was the comment. "You might be better off than us. It's going crazy here. They're expecting a bad flood in town and down at Penzance too, let alone everywhere else. Sandbagging like mad. Wouldn't be the first time we've had to swim to the Coop, but they're saying this could be the worst you and I've ever seen. Try to keep in touch – lifeboats and Air-Sea Rescue are on full alert."

Not ever-so encouraging. Between them they manhandled the invalid into the forward cabin and stretched him out along the worn cushions at one side with a bucket for company.

"'Is mother will never forgive me, bringing him out in this," said Roach, "That's if we all get back in one piece."

Walby put a blanket over the moaning youth.

"Proper job," he commented. "We can both keep an eye on him. Be in some sort of trouble if he choked on it."

Roach nodded. "How's the finger?"

"Sore." Walby was rueful.

"Take six months to knit, that will. Did it myself once."

Jocasta lurched suddenly with a heave of swell. The wind was increasing.

"Are we nearly there yet?" Walby said suddenly, as if he'd been a child on a car trip, and they both laughed, the tension broken.

Outside it had almost stopped raining, Roach noticed. A bit of a blessing. For a couple of minutes he could see clear three or four miles around when they rode out of the troughs. To his north there was only open sea, but to the south there were three large vessels, the nearest a container ship about half a mile away, and like him they were all anchored heading into the wind to ride out the coming storm. Then a band of white mist came up from nowhere and, just as when it had been raining, he could see for no more than three or four hundred yards. The wind fell away just as suddenly as it had blown up, almost nothing, but the deep swell persisted.

"Have we been let off the hook or is it the lull before the storm, d'you think?" He looked at Walby's stubbly face, which was unreadable once again after his recent little flash of humour.

"Reckon," was all the man said, alluding to the latter.

And they sat in silence broken only by an occasional groan from under the blanketed form, and almost playful-sounding slaps of water on *Jocasta's* sturdy wooden flanks, neither of them admitting they were worried about what might be coming at them next.

***

Connor had called the Exeter office from Portishead at midday, and he had been surprised to learn that Mike Winter and Caroline Cleaver were still there – though not on duty and certainly surplus to requirements once all the day shift was in. They told him they had stayed out of fascinated concern about the developing situation. But Connor was having none of that. He insisted they both to go home and have a square meal "and at least a couple of hours' sleep" before reporting back for their evening stint.

The town had geared up rapidly to a full flood alert, they told him. It wasn't the first time there had been local worries about the now overfilled River Exe, or the wide, long, shallow estuary below the town, or both.

"I don't know about you, but I couldn't possibly sleep in these circumstances," Cleaver said as soon as they were out of the door.

"Nor me. No way," Winter agreed. "Let's go for a quick coffee in town anyway. There's nobody at home when I get there, unless they've been sent home. I suppose they could do that to the schoolkids if things look bad – and they were saying something on the news about some schools being evacuation centres. But they need to contact parents first if they shut schools down, of course, to make sure someone's at home." He'd heard nothing about Tom, his 10-year-old, and he was about to call his wife Judy, mainly to see if she was likely to pick the boy up or come home early from her job at the council offices because of the situation – or indeed if there was some other plan. He put the call on hold for the time being, however. He was anxious to see how the town was coping. Cleaver, who had a partner called Palfrey, agreed readily to the coffee plan. Because their ways home were in opposite directions, she accepted his offer of a lift in and then back to the office car park after unwinding with a coffee.

"Plenty of men knit, you know," she confided out of the blue as they drove in. "I could teach you if you like. Palfrey knits."

Winter had a brief vision of the two of them sitting together by their fireside knitting, Palfrey the art gallery co-owner and Caroline, his scientific partner. The concept seemed immediately incongruous, then almost irrepressibly hilarious.

"Mm," he said, turning his head and pretending to look out of the rainswept window, with great difficulty stifling a giggle.

The traffic was ultra-light, but then after one corner they met a small convoy of canvas-covered Army trucks heading in the opposite direction, headlights full on.

"Troops in one, sandbags to the roof in the others," reported Cleaver, who was able to glance over her shoulder into the open-back vehicles. "They look ready for business."

The Costa on the corner in the Princesshay shops was virtually empty when they arrived on foot after parking, having passed a couple of cafes and not a few shops with 'closed' notices on the doors. Normally at this time of the day Costa would be super-busy with queues at the counter. Nor were there many shoppers in the gloom-darkened square outside, but those they did see had laden shopping bags.

"Been like this ever since they put the warnings out," the brown-smocked young barista who made them cappuccinos commented, seeing two more burdened shoppers go past. "People stocking up, food and water. Lots of the other shops have just shut down. It's like there's a war on. Pick a table and I'll bring the drinks over to you."

A radio behind the counter was on loud and tuned to a local station, currently playing a 70s number. "I remember when this area was all little shops," Winter said as they sat down. But Cleaver wasn't really listening, just staring through the plate glass. She suddenly turned, just as the coffees came.

"Well I'm blowed," she said. "You might not believe this, but I think its just stopped raining."

He looked out. Some of the awnings were still dripping but it did indeed seem as if the rain spatters had ceased. He scooped some of the froth off the top of his drink and licked it off his teaspoon, then raised his cup.

"Here's to deliverance ... perhaps!"

Cleaver smiled as they clashed cups.

"Deliverance!"

Chapter 8

"I'll give you a chance to speak to us in a minute or two Mr Connor. Perhaps you can then talk us through the Cobra meeting moves and give us your assessment of what's likely to happen tomorrow morning."

Chief Constable Lees was grim-faced, as were most of the people sitting or standing around the operations table map of Britain showing the snaking Severn and its long, gradually widening estuary, a feature flanked by low-lying land on both the east and west banks. Army chief General Sir Denis Hawling, Michael Saunders of the Environment Agency and others in the 15-strong gathering – firefighter commanders, ambulance and health coordinators, rescue service heads, one of the top men from the NFU – wore head-sets so that they were able to take messages and give orders.

Moving among the principal players were aides who were already beginning to make chart changes with marker pens as the situation developed.

The BBC and other media representatives, eight in all, had been given a table to one side. There were also two TV cameras with cameramen, who had been told they could take only general shots of the operations room for the time being. The Avon and Somerset Police press officer and the Prime Minister's speech-writer had a watching brief in the main party, waiting for guidance on what to put in a press release and, more importantly, what to put in the PM's emergency address to the nation which Connor and Saunders had already been colluding over.

"We've got all our services on full alert, but please try your best to be over-cautious about what might be done to save lives first, property and livestock second," Christine Lees continued. "We've been double-height sandbagging all the major riverside risk points going some way inland from Cornwall and the Gower to as far up the Severn as Worcester, but so far as the Teme goes, a lot of the upstream damage has already been encountered, and there's something else to watch out for from that direction, I believe?"

She got nods from Connor and Saunders.

"And down here," she went on, sweeping her hand down from the Upton-on-Severn hams to Tewkesbury, Gloucester and on to the widening estuary. "Down here, I understand, we'll have the full force of major river overspills combined with an exceptionally high tide driven by a storm surge from Miranda. A lot of that is inevitable I believe. We've already got some overspills from this afternoon's tide which will peak later, but the real problems come on the next tide tomorrow morning.

"We mustn't forget that while this area is especially vulnerable, all areas of Britain's coast where encroachment by the sea is likely will experience varying degrees of risk. The exceptional tide and surge we're expecting will hit us roughly in the St Ives, Porthcurno and Lizard area at the tip of the Cornish peninsula first of all and then progress to us, but it will also push on from Cornwall, branching north up St George's Channel on the one hand and along the English Channel on the other to the North Sea, where it too turns north. The St George's Channel flow will move up and all around the west and north of Scotland, then down the North Sea to meet the upward surge roughly off the English coast near Middlesbrough. Of course, all vulnerable areas have been alerted and are preparing – the Thames Barrage, for example, is having a dummy drill as we speak. Coastal regions of France and the Netherlands further north are also taking action. But hopefully after hitting us the surge will start to dissipate – though we can't be sure of that."

She gestured to Connor to give his contribution.

"That's right," he agreed, giving his beard a final tug and looking round at everyone. Since that morning, he'd been getting used to addressing a largish group of people. It felt like being a teacher, perhaps, or a preacher.

"Thank you, Chief Constable, for such a comprehensive summary. First, I don't want anyone to be under the illusion that this area is facing anything less than a major emergency. I hope you've all looked at the copies of the Severnside paper I've handed around, which is a pretty good account of what happened in a cataclysmic storm-surge in the 17th Century when 2,000 souls were lost and the damage was astronomical, almost unbelievable. If it has happened before, it can happen again. I wouldn't mind betting the meteorological conditions are very similar – unless it really was a tsunami, as has been suggested – but on this occasion we're a bit more ahead of the game than they were back then, and we're not totally unprepared, although there's not much time left to protect everyone.

"As the Chief Constable suggests, this area of the lower Severn and its estuary are in the greatest peril, and I think you should know a few facts that explain why. First and foremost, the Severn Estuary has the third highest tide range – the distance between low and high tides – in the world, beaten only by two locations off the west of North America. On high spring tides, such as the one we are facing, the water can quite normally be expected to rise an incredible fifteen metres, which is damn near fifty feet in old money. Most of you will have heard of the Severn Bore. Because the at-first very wide estuary narrows rapidly and gets progressively shallower as the tide makes its way upstream, it forms a surging shockwave at its front edge, normally a couple of metres high, which travels at around twelve miles an hour – a following wind can make this faster, and other weather conditions can result in a much higher wave. Some unwary spectators on the riverbank get a soaking because they are not aware that the wave itself is not the full height of the tide – the mass of following water goes on rising metres or more until it reaches high tide proper.

"High spring tides are anxious enough times for riverside dwellers, because even in normal times the river overtops flood defences in places. If I add in a factor like the storm surge we are expecting, four, maybe five metres above that, we are looking at something that is unknown here in modern times, and is completely unstoppable – nearly the same set of circumstances, I believe, that led to the Seventeenth Century disaster."

Silence fell across the room. Then the General spoke from his seat with a quiet air of resignation.

"If that means we must take what's coming to us from Miranda, it's now something of a damage limitation exercise. We can't drop a nuclear bomb on her, like Trump once suggested for stopping hurricanes."

Connor looked at him and smiled.

"Damage limitation it is. But on a truly, truly vast scale."

Connor elaborated on his predictions with an explanation of the Rule of Twelfths, the mariners' scale for measuring the way tides flow, peaking at high water and falling back to low tide. From every low tide, the rise begins slowly during the first hour, increasing at hourly intervals until, after six hours, the flow slows then ceases at high water. After a short slack period the water begins to fall once again and run in the opposite direction if there is a tidal current or if the tide has filled a bay or estuary. A chart of this movement over a twelve-hour period would look like a roller-coaster.

He drew a large 'X' at the tip of the Cornish peninsula to mark his starting point.

"I'm trying to time everything as I go," he explained. "Here we are at zero, low water if you like, and the tide is just about to start running. It's about 3am, but perhaps a bit earlier because it will be driven by the very high winds we're expecting around then. Luckily, most of the North Cornwall coast and North Devon for that matter is rugged with high cliffs, although harbours and river mouths – places like Barnstaple, for example – are of course preparing for the worst."

He drew an amoeba-like outline from Westward Ho! on the coast to skirt the Torridge mouth and the long Taw estuary stretching well inland past the town of Barnstaple and its historic multi-arched Taw Bridge, shaded it in with cross-hatching. Aides were at the same time marking out other low-lying areas to the south-west and to the north of Westward Ho! that would also be facing extreme tidal incursions, but apart from Connor's voice and the occasional trill of a phone and muted responses, the atmosphere in the almost-silent room was tense.

"Minutes are passing as the surge grows. The tide has already risen by a considerable amount by the time it starts affecting the Somerset coast – by now it's getting on for 5am. It's starting to behave more like a real monster too. The wind has increased to Force10 or even 11 on the Beaufort Scale and the waves are short but frighteningly steep. It's no time to be out at sea. There's a rain front riding on it too so there will probably be lashing rain and hail – quite likely thunder too. You could be forgiven for saying it seems apocalyptic.

"Try to think of the surge as a huge hump of water being drawn up by the moon's gravitational pull in the Atlantic off the west coast of Ireland – water that would rather be flat and level, but for the moment can't subside. Tonne after metric tonne of it. As a normal tide, it would start to flow away towards our shores, raising the water levels up to high tide. However, in this case the 'hump' is a great deal bigger than usual, and it's driven on by a severe gale that is starting to move it en masse towards the south of Ireland and towards Cornwall – but most of all towards the coasts of Devon and Somerset."

He started to draw a series of Xs from North Devon moving upwards towards their own position in the police HQ at Portishead beside the confluence of the Bristol Avon with the Severn Estuary.

"And this is the seaward boundary of the area that will first bear the full brunt of the beast – much of it extremely low-lying reclaimed marshland that has flooded in the past and even in more recent times. Broadly it's the huge basin between the Mendip Hills just outside Bristol down to the Quantocks and the edge of Exmoor in the south, some of it known as the Somerset Levels. And we expect all of this…"

Here Connor drew an enormous scoop inland from the Mendips down past Bridgewater and hatched it in.

"We expect all of this to go under by, say, 6am tomorrow, to varying degrees – fields, farms, houses, villages, everything. And it's the most sensitive part of the problem because once the water is in situ, as it were, there are very few ways to clear it all out again quickly, as the disastrous Somerset floods of 2013-14 showed. It won't just run away the next day."

"Is it really as much as that?" an ambulance chief interrupted. "Are you sure we aren't exaggerating the problem?"

That 'exaggerating' word again. Another doubter. Connor paused and looked at him levelly, then said gravely: "I'm very sorry to say, for those of you who haven't quite grasped the severity of the threat we are facing, that this…" He knocked his knuckles on the shaded area of Somerset, "…this is only one small part of the overall situation."

Drawing rapidly with the marker he moved to the Welsh side of the estuary and hatched in areas behind Cardiff Bay, including low areas of the city of Cardiff itself, on up past Newport, over the Gwent Levels up to the rising land that housed Wentwood Reservoir, past Chepstow and over the flat land below the Forest of Dean and, with a few 'islands' of high land like Newnham and Westbury, all the way to Gloucester – the higher parts of this town also one of the 'islands'. He drew no upward edge to the hatched area past Gloucester, but started moving down from the other bank including the city's broad flood plain hams and, lower, the entire Arlingham Loop, the flat lands cradled by the Cotswold Edge including Slimbridge and the old nuclear power stations at Berkeley and Oldbury, and on to North and West Bristol, ending back at Portishead. He started putting times against the marked areas.

"As you can see, this is our immediate problem. There's more still to come on the higher river in addition to Michael Saunders' outlines, but I'll leave that for the moment.

"Right, once our monster surge inundates the Somerset coast, it continues upriver while some of it washes back to the other side of the Severn – Cardiff, Chepstow and beyond – to cover any low-lying land. In all, I reckon we're looking at about several hundred square miles of floods, just in these areas alone."

Another question interrupted him, this time from a Government representative.

"What sort of wave levels are we looking at? On the overflowing water, I mean. Will it actually be a wave?"

Connor stifled a sigh. People were obsessed with waves, it seemed to him.

"Inland, it will be more like the tide coming in at Weston, for those of you who are familiar with that, or anywhere else where the tide draws out a long way – remember the Morecambe Bay cockle-pickers tragedy? At low tide you can walk several hundred yards from the beach, but when the tide turns it's just an approaching trickle at first, albeit moving quite quickly. Anyone who knows that sign would turn and head for the shore at a high rate of knots, but the unwary who stay soon realise that the water is all around them and deepening quickly while the 'trickle' they though was harmless is now a long way behind them. There's never been any indication of a wave. Many get trapped – there have been lots of drownings over the years.

"Your 'waves' as such are more prevalent where they hit steep beaches and cliffs – or breakwaters, which in this instance we expect to be overtopped. Perhaps Mr Saunders is better informed than I am about the state of our current flood defences? And I'm sure he can give us a clear picture of what we might expect further up our river systems?"

Saunders stood and cleared his throat. He was a tall presence, calm and collected.

"I'm aware some of you might think the Environment Agency is at fault for a lot of what is about to happen," he said. "But our brief in recent years, and certainly after the last Somerset floods, has been to make sure our flood banks and river depths are up to the sorts of storms we might expect every twenty or so years, but as Mr Connor points out, the danger we are facing now is unprecedented in modern times – I suppose the Seventeenth Century disaster is the nearest we come to it. Extrapolating from that I'd like to be able to say we don't expect anything of this nature every three to five hundred years or so, but with the man-made pressure on our weather and sea levels I can't be anything like certain it can't happen again soon, or more frequently. In short, because you'll all be worried about the here and now, we simply can't rely on most of our present floodbank defences. They aren't up to it. We've done what we can with the money that has been made available to us, but it's nowhere near adequate.

"I have three major concerns in the current situation. One is here…" he pointed to the hatching around Shrewsbury, "…and the other is the River Teme, above Worcester – here."

All the watermeadows that normally flooded in heavy rains were full up, he told them. The recent extremely heavy rain was now moving down the rivers of the Severn catchment like swellings in its major veins – chiefly on the Severn itself, the Teme joining at Worcester, the Warwickshire Avon joining at

Tewkesbury, the Bristol Avon flowing right under their noses at Portishead and the Wye opposite them on the Welsh bank.

"On the Teme we have third problem. Overnight on the upper reaches it became dammed by a variety of circumstances and is shifting a huge amount of debris at its forward edge. Already this has taken out bridges – some of them vital crossings – and forced several people from their homes. We're expecting all that to arrive in the Worcester area at almost exactly the same time as the heavy floodwater coming down the Severn from Shrewsbury. Combined, this will flow on downriver – first to Tewkesbury, then to Gloucester. Unhappily, it will arrive at Tewkesbury at just about the time the storm surge is coming upstream tomorrow morning. Much of what happens then depends on the force and extent of the incursion. But we are looking at a huge area generally known as the Severn Vale, between the Malverns on the one hand and the Cotswolds on the other, being inundated, along with land to either side of the Warwickshire Avon, perhaps even as high as Stratford and beyond. Tewkesbury, we believe, is particularly vulnerable. Historically it has always borne the brunt of flooding. And if I lived in Gloucester I'd be pretty worried too."

Chapter 9

Nobody could say that any stones were left unturned as the Portishead HQ cadre attended to the emergency measures that sprang from the predictions laid before them.

The decommissioned nuclear power stations at Oldbury and Berkeley in Gloucestershire as well as the larger nuclear sites at Hinkley A and Hinkley B down on the Somerset coast received special attention. Teams of bulldozers and JCBs were rapidly commandeered and set to work in the rain to shore up high banks around them. Similar protection was also being given to electricity sub-stations and domestic water plants.

Although the protection of people was the main concern, the NFU chief was worried about stock, and chiefly milking cows. Sure, they could be moved to higher ground, and there wasn't a landowner in the country with elevated land who didn't offer it up for this purpose – but the animals also needed milking regularly. If this didn't happen, they could easily develop an udder condition called mastitis, which was painful and sometimes fatal, or dry up and give no more milk. The NFU was given emergency powers to requisition whatever was needed, from cattle trucks to move animals to mobile milking parlours. The farmers' organisation also put out a general appeal, widely picked up in the media, for anyone with hand-milking experience to offer their help if called upon. Nobody mentioned there was no marketing structure for the milk produced and most of it would have to be poured away.

Hospitals and ambulance services were put on standby and all staff leave was cancelled. The same applied to the Police, the Army and military and civilian rescue helicopters. Several helicopters were being flown from the rest of the country to Bristol airport, high in the Mendips, which was now closed to civilian flights. Buses had been commandeered and were starting to ferry people, particularly inhabitants of nursing and old people's homes, to safe areas.

The last but perhaps the most important items on the agenda were the questions of how long the emergency might last, and what measures should be taken for the recovery.

They were just wrapping these preliminaries up when Connor had a call from his superior in Exeter, Marion Cooper. He had been wondering why he hadn't heard from the Met Office chief so far. She was a likeable woman, if inclined to be brisk, and young for such a responsible job. But super-bright, as her nickname inferred.

"Marion?"

"Good Morning, Mervyn, if it is still morning. Can you give me a quick roundup of where we are? I've been busy keeping the shop going here and I can see what the weather's like without knowing what people like you are doing about it, know what I mean? And there have been a lot of interruptions, mainly from politicians, wouldn't you guess. Fill me in."

He gave her the story so far and she thanked him when he was done, but she finished with a caveat.

"Look, there's a growing political aspect to all this which you ought to be aware of. We must talk about that some time when you get free of fighting on the front. I'm sure some of the dunderheads around us think we created this storm rather than predicting its progress. If you have any public announcements to make on the situation, can you run them past me first please? I've a feeling we all need to be sure we're singing from the same hymn book."

***

Not everyone in the world was buying the 'impending disaster' story in the same spirit, among them surfer Alan Jenkins, aka 'Jinkin' Jenkins'. He had been a Severn bore surfboard-rider all his life – well, for as long as he'd mastered the technique at the age of 16. That was 20 years ago, and he'd been perfecting the art ever since. He'd ridden all kinds of bores in all kinds of weather, in the dark and under blazing sun, and he'd also been abroad to ride the giant bores like the 'killer' on the Qiantang River in China, among others. Sometimes on his home patch the Severn Bore was a tame little beast and sometimes it could be a roaring monster, but he was regarded as a local specialist in getting the best from all situations, and he wasn't going to let this major one go past without having a crack at it.

The police, of course, had other ideas. The word was getting around that any bore riding in this situation was strictly off limits.

In the past Alan had been pictured many times in the papers and on television as the archetypal board expert, able to judge better than most others where the leading wave would arrive first, skipping in across the sand flats below the little town of Newnham, where he lived not far from the settlement's distinctive church on the crest of a riverside knoll. As the board and canoe riders lined up for any predicted big bore, he'd be lying on his belly to wait for the rumble and crunch of the approaching wild water, and then paddling strongly with his arms to get up to speed, catch the wave. And more often than not he'd be the first up on his feet, a tall, flying figure in his wet suit, bandana-tied hair streaming behind, heading round the broad Arlingham loop and on to Minsterworth below Gloucester, where it arrived with a great roar about an hour later. A seven-mile ride is the best recorded and although he wasn't the record-holder, Alan had often come close to that goal. Like the others caught up in the excitement, he sometimes recalled the heroic exploits of Colonel 'Mad' Jack

Churchill who dared to ride the wave on a home-made board back in 1955. Highly-decorated soldier Jack, generally reckoned to be the first of the modern riders, was also renowned for wearing a claymore into battle in both world wars ("Any officer who goes into battle without his sword is not properly dressed."), although the tale that he actually killed an enemy soldier with a longbow arrow is probably apocryphal. Of late the bores had become quite a spectator attraction, with watchers entertained by riders in fancy dress including, at one time, a whole brigade of them swooping upriver dressed as star ship troopers. But Alan wasn't in it because he was an exhibitionist – he did it because he loved it.

Alan had risen late that morning, coming round after a heavy night with old friends. When he heard the news and the warnings about the surge, his first thought was to ring John Carter at the *Clarion*. John was an old friend. Alan had often been on the front page of the paper for his bore exploits. Annoyingly, John had gone home, he learned. That didn't matter so much – he had his home landline number.

It rang some time before it was answered.

"Yes? What is it?"

At first Alan did not catch the tetchiness in the voice.

"John – I'm going to ride this wave in the morning. Can you set up some pictures?"

There was a pause. Then a flat voice:

"You can't. You'll be killed you silly bugger. Don't do it."

"But I must. And I will...you all right, by the way? Something upset you?"

"Not really."

"What then?"

Another pause. Then: "Oh, just a bit of bother, that's all. Nothing you've done. Look, this surge isn't going to be the sort of animal you think it is. Everyone's really worried about it. I'd have a good long think about it if I were you – and if any other silly sods are thinking of doing it, I hope you'll tell them the same. And I'll have to wash my hands of you. I can't encourage it."

"But you'll send Tad Morgan to Newnham to get pictures, eh?"

Pause.

"Maybe."

And the line went dead.

Alan thought about how dangerous his plan might be for a good twenty seconds. Then he went out to his work shed to wax his board.

***

On their hill farm Alice and Owen James heard of the alarming downriver progress of the Teme floodwater on the kitchen radio at around midday. They had been trying to complete the Jumbo crossword from last Saturday's newspaper, but stopped to listen to the bulletin. The flood had reached the Knighton area, they learned, after it had overtopped bridges and banks and inundated countless acres of low-lying farmland. For many in Knighton, and for large areas upstream of that, the warnings had come too late to make many preparations. The water was already lapping up town streets and making its way into homes and businesses. It was clear a lot of properties had suffered and floorboarding carpeting, furniture and everything that hadn't been quickly shifted upstairs would be ruined. But thankfully, so far, nobody in the little settlement at the junction of the Glyndwr Way and Offas's Dyke walking trails had been physically harmed.

So far, the water was still running in a stop-start fashion as uprooted trees and other debris at the leading edge met any obstructions, inevitably ripping some of these into the watercourse. The area Environment Agency had quickly mobilised gangs to try to keep the whole of this mass moving while snatching anything they could grab with boathooks out of the seething mess if it got snagged up. It was dirty and dangerous work, the local press officer reported, but there were plenty of volunteers who joined in to help. A huge amount of water was penned up behind the rolling dam, and there was no way they would ever unplug it enough to get it flowing more easily. But from the bridge at Dutlas and down through Knighton they did at least feel they were helping it on its way.

Below, where the swollen River Clun joined the Teme from the north at Leintwardine, the water would at last be able to spread itself over a larger area, slow down a bit and dump some of its load as a long, wide lake formed. However, when the valley narrowed again it was expected to once more become a fast and angry flood heading for Ludlow, Tenbury Wells and, finally Worcester and the Severn – but it would not reach these places any time soon.

"Oh, poor devils!" Alice Jones commented in sympathy for those in the flood's path. "To think, it all started up here. Do you think that without that tree rolling down last night it might not have been so bad?"

Owen shrugged.

"No way of telling, is there? There's been a mighty lot of rain anyway. I don't suppose it helped."

The news bulletin was a long one and it had already run over its time. The next item was an appeal from the Environment Agency for more volunteers to help with the downstream flood relief work. Owen looked at his wife without saying anything, but she knew he was feeling helpless. A man with a gammy leg would be of little use to them. She reached across the table for his hand and gave it a comforting squeeze.

Then came a surprise. The NFU apparently needed anyone with hand-milking experience to help with cows being evacuated from the lower Severn ahead of widespread flooding expected that night, along with a big tidal surge in some areas.

Owen's face lit up.

"Now there's something I *can* do," he said.

The radio fell silent and crackled while he was jotting the NFU coordinator's contact number down at the edge of the crossword page, and then a new voice suddenly broke in.

"*This is the BBC. Please keep your radio or television switched on for a following important announcement by the Prime Minister.*"

In common with millions of people throughout the nation, Owen felt a sudden chill. In all his born days, he'd never heard a statement like that before.

***

It was raining cats and dogs in Downing Street, but although the Prime Minister had been advised she didn't need to step outside to deliver the speech that had been sent from Bristol, she chose to brave the weather. The squally deluge, she told her aides, would add atmosphere and relevance to the statement – a document that had been quickly knocked into shape with input from Connor, Saunders and the various emergency services. It had to paint the looming problem in broad brushstrokes, she had briefed the writer, avoiding too much minor detail. All the minutiae could be supplied by the string of contact numbers relevant to particular areas and concerns that would follow the announcement. Nevertheless, it had to transmit, in a nutshell, the full gravity of the situation.

Despite the wet she faced a barrage of cameras and microphones as she walked the few steps from the door of Number 10 to the podium. She wore a business-like navy two-piece suit with white trim around the lapels and hem, black high heel shoes and a single-string pearl necklace. Her carefully coiffured was immediately given lift and volume by the wind as she stood under a large umbrella held high above her by an aide. Her notes were already clipped on the lectern.

"*People of Britain…*" she started, followed by a frustrated yelp from somebody who had not yet set his camera running. She waited for his nod.

"*People of Britain…* (another pause) *People of Britain, I am making this address because we are facing perhaps one of the worst crises since the last World War. During the coming night one of the severest storm surges our country has ever known is expected to collide with our South Western shores. The tidal wave* (She'd fought to use the word 'wave' rather than Connor's suggested 'surge' because, she thought, it added impact) *backed by storm-force winds is almost certain to breach our sea defences from early tomorrow morning and inundate large areas of low-lying ground.*

"*Not only that, but the persistent heavy rain of recent days has saturated the ground and filled rivers to overflowing in many areas. Tidal influences will make a problem we already have become a good deal worse.*

"*While North Devon, Somerset, Gloucestershire and Gwent are most at risk, the Severn Vale and all parts of the coast are expecting exceptionally high tides. It is therefore vital first of all to see if any vulnerable people are unprotected, in order to move them from harm's way, and secondly to make no unnecessary road journeys so that emergency services can move freely. People should also keep well away from sea walls, piers and any places exposed to the sea, and that applies all round the coast. The safest place will be indoors until all danger is past, which will be tomorrow afternoon. Even the next day, perhaps.*"

Pause to take a sip of water offered at her elbow. She cleared her throat, started again.

"*I'm appealing for anyone with experience of emergencies to put themselves forward if they think they can help – you may be a retired nurse or firefighter, for example – and the telephone numbers and email addresses for contacts will be given after this bulletin as well as on the BBC news site for the rest of today.*

"*If you are in any of the danger zones, or if you know people, particularly vulnerable people, who might be in danger, the contacts are also being given. Likewise, if you can offer any help, perhaps billeting someone on a temporary basis, please also make yourself known.*

"All schools and colleges will be closed until the all-clear is given, probably on the day after tomorrow. Companies can decide whether or not they wish to keep on working, but I will re-state the general advice is for everyone to stay safely at home until all danger from Storm Miranda and the tidal surge is past."

The Prime Minister waved away questions, turned and retreated to enter the famous black door, which briefly opened and immediately shut behind her.

On both BBC television channels as well as ITV and satellite stations the PM's speech had gone out live. While ITV afterwards resumed their normal programming, the BBC cut to live shots of the operations room in Bristol, then interviewed Chief Constable Lees, who gave a brief account of the preparations so far. Before going back to their own programming, the BBC set up a repeating ribbon showing emergency telephone numbers that would stay on the bottom of viewers' screens throughout the crisis.

All the daily newspapers were in turmoil. The worst effects of Storm Miranda and the tidal surge flooding would be felt after they had already gone to press. That was a newsman's nightmare.

Chapter 10

Colin Roach and his two companions aboard the scallop-dredger *Jocasta* were among the first people to experience the opening overtures from Miranda.

As Roach and the injured Walby had feared, the windless lull was short-lived, and as if it had taken a long, deep breath to gather strength, the worsening weather announced its return with a sudden squall and a thunderclap, followed by drumming rain so furious that it actually flattened out the wave crests.

"Glory be!" said Walby. "Now we're in for it."

The sky darkened by several shades and the wind started to whistle around them. *Jocasta* easily crested the first wave that gave her a caressing, almost playful slap. Then the vessel sank giddily into a deep trough. The water behind them was now as high as the next wave ahead.

"Sod," said Roach. "Too much of this and we'll all join young Jago in the sick-room."

"Or in Davey Jones' Locker," was Walby's grim addition as they rose again, this time high enough to see one big wave after another straight ahead and rolling swiftly towards them. He clutched the wheel with his good hand. At the wave's peak, *Jocasta* gave a little twist and they felt a grating vibration as the anchor line was snatched tight. The sick boy lying on the cubby seat rolled a little with the movement. He was unconscious now, having worn himself out with constant retching. Fortunately the movement wasn't enough to roll him onto the floor, Roach was glad to see. And he knew that if *Jocasta* could take one big wave, she could probably take many more. Provided things didn't get very much worse, that was.

Down they went again, then up, and this time he engaged the engine to help his boat climb. But the peak came up far too quickly and the engine raced as *Jocasta* twisted again and put her nose down into the trough and the screw came out of the water to bite on empty air, screaming – and far too close to the anchor line. Not a good idea, the engine, so he disengaged it but once again kept it running.

At the top of the next wave, Walby said he thought the grating sound they heard over the engine noise might be the anchor dragging. Roach nodded agreement.

"I'd say it might be, but just a bit. We can go a long way like that without any trouble so long as we don't snag a wreck. But have you noticed our anchor rope is going almost straight down now? It's as if we've either come into a deep bit of ground or we're riding on another forty feet or so of water. I can't afford to put more rope onto the anchor but the old way of keeping us from going head over arse might work – trailing something over the stern ramp to keep a drag on the back. There's our old trawl net in the port locker back there. Do you think we could get it over between us?"

Walby grinned.

"Only one way to find out."

The dense cloud cover made it black as night in between brilliant bursts of sheet lightning as the two men made their way, bare heads bent into the weather, along the bucking, slopping deck to the stern lockers. Just as much water was coming aboard from the wind-lashed waves as from the deluge, and Walby almost lost his footing more than once, but Roach had insisted they were both fixed at the waist to ropes tied to a forward deck stanchion. If they slipped down there was something to haul themselves back up with. It was impossible to speak – any sound was torn out of their mouths, and they had to communicate as best they could with gestures.

They started to struggle with the hatch-cover catches. Roach thought they were probably nearing the centre of the storm, if they weren't there already, but he had no idea how long this phase might last. The wind had now turned cyclonic, going every which-way, and there were bursts of stinging hail mixed with the howling air, turning to slush when it collected on the deck making it even more slippery. But perhaps an hour might see them through the worst of it, provided they could stay afloat. With the catches open they both gripped the locker rim, made ready to haul it open on a bawled count of three.

The wind caught the opening lid, ripped it out of their fingers and it flew back to crash onto the deck. They exchanged glances of gratitude. If anybody had been in the way of that, they could have been badly hurt. Then they reached in and began to unfurl the neatly stowed netting. Roach, who had two good hands, took the ends of the two net lines to lash them securely to the sturdy iron frame of Jocasta's stern winch while Walby piled the netting on the stern ramp. Then, each of them holding tightly onto a winch leg, they raised boots and kicked it bodily into the water. Within a minute the ropes jerked tight suddenly and Jocasta, on her way up another monster wave slope, shuddered, then steadied.

It seemed to have done the trick. There was no time to congratulate each other. They made their way back along the deck, gripping tightly onto their safety lines. When they were back in the cubby at last, they were glad to see Jago was still sleeping peacefully, oblivious to the storm.

"Lucky little bugger," Walby commented.

"Ay," agreed Roach. "But we're not home and dry yet, are we?"

The VHF radio crackled suddenly, and Roach picked up the handset. Newlyn. He threw a switch. "Aye," he said, "*Jocasta.*"

"How are you doing?"

Not Harry's voice.

"Well as can be expected, but we're still here. You?"

"*Jocasta*, we have a mayday near you. Container ship *Anita*, listing heavily from shifting cargo. Crewed by 14, including Captain Julian Cais, Dutchman. Two overboard. Can you assist?"

Roach looked at Walby, his eyes wide. "*Overboard*?" he exclaimed aloud, "*In this*? Poor bastards!"

He replied to Newlyn: "OK, we'll see if we can do anything, but it'll have to be after we're through the blow. I know there's one container vessel out near us, like, and it could be *Anita*, but it's lousy as 'ell now and we can't see a blind thing through the rain. It's hard enough keeping us all safe. I'll go straight to Channel 16, see if we can hear anything from them…"

Then an afterthought: "Who am I speaking to, by the way?"

"John Cook, Harry's son. Dad's gone to help with the lifeboat."

Roach knew Cook's boy. "They're launching, Johno?" he asked.

"They're launching."

"Tell Harry 'good luck' from me."

Roach took *Anita*'s coordinates, cut the call and switched to the emergency frequency. He turned grim-faced and said to Walby "Oh my dear Lord. I hope this isn't another bloody Penlee in the making."

Walby, equally grim, nodded but said nothing. They both knew the story. The Penlee Lifeboat Disaster had affected almost everyone in the south west of Cornwall, which was a close-knit community. In 1981 on December 19 the Penlee boat that served the Newlyn area was launched in heavy seas and hurricane-force winds to go to the assistance of coaster *Union Star*, which was drifting helplessly eight miles off the Wolf Rock. Her engines had failed. Battling huge odds seven volunteers and coxswain William Richards took the *Solomon*

Browne alongside the stricken vessel and began the struggle to bring its crew and three passengers – the captain's wife and their two teenage daughters – aboard. Lifeboat coxswain William Richards sent a message ashore that they had rescued four. That was the last that was heard from either crew. Not all the bodies were recovered.

Since the disaster, a new (and larger) craft bought by public subscription had been stationed in Newlyn harbour but it is still called the Penlee Lifeboat, and the town's Christmas lights are always turned off on December 19 in respect for the lost souls. And nobody has ever forgiven the Thatcher government of the day that tried to tax the public collection money until a wave of disapproval forced a U-turn.

***

The captain of Nassau-registered *Anita*, like most of his countrymen, had excellent English. The Bay Class ship was 900ft overall and could carry 4000 TEUs (Twenty-foot Equivalent Units) the figure representing 4000 standard shipping containers. When the bad weather struck they had 3700 TEUs aboard and were on their way from Panama to Rotterdam. They were looking forward to entering the English Channel, unloading and enjoying a bit of shore R&R while they were re-loaded before setting off again for Central America – a familiar run for them. The containers held mostly American cars and car parts and also fancy footwear, bottled edible oil and tinned meats from Brazil. There were five deck officers, nearly all Europeans, a Dutch engineer and seven Filipino hands including the cook.

When he heard the forecast, Captain Julian Cais knew that the channel ahead would be crammed with vessels scurrying for safe harbours. Dangerous at the best of times, it would be doubly dangerous soon. He'd be heading into this at quite a late hour almost on the wings of the storm. Deciding it wouldn't be worth the risk, he'd come about to anchor up and ride out the bad weather where there were not so many potential dangers. They struck a brief lull, but he could see a band of dark cloud coming in fast, so he felt glad he had made this choice – *Anita* had often faced enormous waves in storms out on the open Atlantic. Scanning round as the vessel settled, he saw a scallop trawler had also anchored a good half a mile to starboard, while a similar distance away to port was a Navy oiler, also sitting tight.

Making decisions like this reminded him of his early days of captaincy, when his skill and judgement were relied on to safely deliver a cargo. Nowadays, he could programme the ship's computer in Sydney, say, press a button and retire below with the rest of the crew to drink endless cups of tea, play cards and watch videos until they were sailing into the destination port.

But then the wind and rain had ramped up suddenly and violently and the ship ploughed into a series of steep roller-coaster swells. *Anita* dug her prow in under the foot of one of these while her stern was still riding high on the previous wave, lurching to port as she did so and plunging the foredeck with its stacked container cargo deep under the surface.

From the high aft bridge, the captain saw a monster wave crest surging towards him across the tops of the containers, covering them in a boil of foam. That alone would not have worried him too unduly, but a sudden dull 'clunk' that reverberated throughout the ship really was something to be concerned about. Moments later, to his utter astonishment, an unattached bright orange container bobbed up through the seething water. As the rest of the vessel emerged, he saw to his dismay that almost all of two rows of port-side containers, all 40-footers and four tiers deep, were missing. Some were floating beside the ship like rubber ducks in a bath, and some were slowly sinking. Four of the units dangled precariously half over the edge. To Cais, who had never yet lost a container (although there were many similar ships that did), this was a disaster.

With rising panic, he hit the alarm klaxon button, then did his best to calm himself down, keep a clear head and sort out the situation as best as he and the crew were able. But luck was not on his side because after righting herself, *Anita* slowly but surely started to roll over onto her starboard side, where the cargo weight was now concentrated. They were heeling over, in worsening weather. The 'disaster' had taken another unexpected turn. There was a very real danger they could capsize, particularly if they took in any water. Was that likely? Not if all the hatches and internal doors were shut, and not if the hull was undamaged – but that was an unknown quantity, because one of the heavy containers could easily have gashed *Anita* below the waterline.

Cais called his deck officers for reports, wondering what had gone wrong. It was hard to believe any of the interlocking corners of the containers had been left undone. Indeed, he'd made it his business to inspect them all as the load grew. No, it must have started with one of them breaking, sheering under severe strain, and weakening the integrity of the whole stack. But there was little time for an inquest now. He needed to keep his men safe, first and foremost, and the ship and what was left of its cargo, for all it was worth, came justifiably second.

He ordered the first-deck officer up to the severely sloping bridge for a hasty consultation, and asked him to look through the hail-rattled pane at the damage and at *Anita*'s increasing degree of list.

"What do you think? Could we go under?"

The man surveyed the situation white-faced and didn't take long to come to a conclusion. He nodded.

"In these seas, a big chance, especially if we're holed."

"Mayday – you agree?"

Another nod. Cais hurriedly sent out a mayday call, asked for all their six regulation lifeboats to be made ready and ordered everyone to put on their buoyancy aids and be prepared. He got the engineer to start the engines and test if they would have any headway if they tried to run for a safe harbour, Cork or perhaps a hospitality berth in Port Talbot – provided *Anita* did not roll over or start sinking in the meantime, that was. She'd need enough power for steerage in a following sea.

"If we all keep our heads, we'll get out of this safely," he said – more to convince himself than encourage anyone else.

Then came a fraught call from the officer overseeing the plated cargo deck. Three men who had been wrestling to secure a container had been swept over the side with it. They quickly had a line to one of them, and had hauled him up unharmed, but his companions had floated away and were now well astern. Whether or not they were still managing to hold on to the container nobody could tell. In deteriorating visibility the men and the big iron box were quickly out of sight.

Reaction to the Mayday was quick. The Penlee lifeboat announced it was preparing to launch. The Welsh salvage tug *Afon Wen*, returning from a barge-towing operation in the north Bristol Channel, radioed she was already at sea and on her way. She was about two hours away, perhaps a bit more in these conditions. Would they like a tow?

Cais gave an update, saying he was particularly concerned about the men adrift with a container. But there were no onboard casualties, he was glad to report. It was a relief to know the lifeboat was on its way but he had to be careful about taking assistance from a salvage vessel, for the cost to his consortium of owners could be high. Such transactions were carried out on a 'no win, no fee' basis but if the salvage was successful the tug men would claim 'a reward commensurate with the value of the cargo'. There was no time, obviously, to consult the consortium on this matter – he was the master, and it was his call. He asked the tug to stand by for the time being and said he would try to limp to port unaided. To risk turning to look for the lost crewmen and put everyone else at risk was unhappily out of the question: a God-fearing man, he said a prayer for their safety – if they were alive. What they might be going through he could not imagine.

The engineer reported both screws were still in the water and therefore operable, but the port bow-thruster was halfway exposed and useless.

"Very well. Bring in our anchor and we'll start to turn about wide," Cais said, planning a course for Cork as his best bet. With luck, if they made it there safely, they'd be able to rearrange what was left of the containers and continue with the ship righted. The safety of the crew, his main priority, was another matter. All the remaining men were well but naturally scared in the circumstances. Even if the Penlee lifeboat reached them, ship-to-ship transfers would be extremely risky The rescue team's best bet would be to stand off in readiness in case Cais and his men had to abandon ship entirely.

A message came in from the nearby Navy oiler to say she had *Anita* on radar. The captain said they would edge as close as possible and keep her company if she was trying a run for port, but would have to keep well away from any hazards. Like the Penlee lifeboat, they were added insurance in case the *Anita* went down. They were also scanning for any signs of the lost container and the two men overboard.

Then the little fishing boat that Cais had last seen on their other flank also radioed in.

"Hello *Anita*. This is the fishing boat *Jocasta*. We're not far off you and we're upping anchor and starting to run down the weather off your stern to see if we can locate your men on the container. Good luck."

Chapter 11

Far away from dramas at sea, Britain's landlubbers were preparing desperately for the coming storm. Mass evacuations had taken place in most of the locations expected to be exposed to tidal influxes as well as to river flooding. A huge number of vulnerable houses had had to be abandoned, while in others the inhabitants had moved everything possible to upper floors and were preparing to sit it out with grandstand views from bedroom windows.

Shops and stores experienced a sudden run on essentials. Stocks of bottled water, milk, bread and baked beans in particular were being snapped up in anticipation of coming shortages and it wasn't long before 'Sold Out' signs for these items were going up all over the place. Candles too were popular. Warnings of possible power cuts were being given on radio and TV, along with advice like keeping freezers tightly shut and being careful with oil and bottled gas heating and lamps because of both the fire risk and carbon monoxide poisoning.

The water companies were filling bowsers in case pumping systems failed, and the National Grid and telephone companies had put all their repair and maintenance teams on full alert until the crisis was over, whenever that might be.

Many businesses, including shops and stores, were already closing early, sending their staff home. Schools that hadn't already closed were sending children back home or making sure they were somewhere safe until parents could collect them.

Companies running the Irish, English Channel and North Sea ferry crossings announced they would cease operations from 7pm that evening, well ahead of the 'most at risk' period, and they were telling freight companies to delay trips 'possibly as long as 48 hours, maybe more'. Lorries already heading for ports were being advised to find secure parking, or stack along emergency lanes being created on some motorways under the direction of local police. The ferries themselves were either tying up or intending to hold position in deep and relatively safe water offshore. Other boats, small and large, in sea harbours and anchorages were made as secure as it was possible – the same went for craft along vulnerable inland waterways. Where possible, many had been hauled up on dry land. Practically every owner was worried. Nobody could tell how destructive the surge would be, or exactly how far the water could rise.

There was much anxious checking of the small print on insurance policies...

***

By late afternoon, John Carter had heard nothing from Phyllis. She wasn't answering her mobile phone. For all he knew she was well on her way to her parents in Bath, but she would have had to be lucky to get that far because the radio news was reporting there were already a lot of road closures in addition to the car bans on the Severn crossings. Phyllis's stated intention to try to get through 'round the back of Cinderford' had been a good one, because there she would be on a ridge. But there would be problems, perhaps, at Gloucester, where roads – and bridges in particular – were always at risk. Still, if she got over the Severn there she could strike for the higher ground of the Cotswolds where roads along the edge would get her safely all the way to her stated objective, if that really was where she was going.

Carter felt sick of the situation. The excitement of bringing out a special edition about the flood had faded fast. Now he tried to analyse what had brought him to this point in his domestic life, a runaway wife, or apparently so.

He had no idea whether she intended their separation to be permanent. To make matters worse, she had 'pinched' his company Fiesta.

The land line phone rang, and he pounced on it, hoping it was her. But no, it was only Tad Morgan. The photographer told him he was in Newnham, beside the Severn, but said he was going to come in and download some flood pictures at the office.

"Can't really rely on phones. Sixes and sevens – I only just got through to you after four or five goes."

"Newnham? What have you been doing there?"

"Mainly trying to persuade that dip-stick Alan Jenkins that riding a storm surge on a surfboard doesn't sound like a very good idea. But he's got these sort of, you know, *staring mad* eyes. Him and his pals too."

"There's more of them?"

"About half a dozen. The police are talking with them now. The surfers are saying they can't be stopped, it's a free country and if they want to kill themselves, well, that's their business. Know what I mean?"

"They *will* be killed."

"They'll probably all be killed," agreed Tad in voice that sounded as if nothing could be done about it. "Now, do you want me to drop round after I've downloaded my stuff? You're coming across a little bit down. A pint, perhaps?"

"Huh!" Carter exclaimed. "Photography and psychology. What talents you have. I'll clear my couch."

"No need to be sarky," Tad said, adding: "Great special edition, by the way. You know they've all gone, sold out, don't you? At least they are this way."

And he rang off. Carter lay back in his chair and closed his eyes. He had felt a cold wall growing between himself and Phyllis over the last couple of months. Yet every time he'd asked her if anything was wrong, she had been evasive. Perhaps it was his working odd hours. She'd known that would be the case when they married four years ago, hadn't she? Long days editing, covering the evening council meetings, football (not her thing) or a rugby match, sometimes both, at weekends. Had his job perhaps turned her into a grass widow?

Or maybe it was the children thing. She wanted one, possibly two, and he hadn't objected. Hardly his fault that this had not happened yet. All the same, if he couldn't produce one for her, maybe somebody else could? But who? There had been no inkling of anyone else in her life, but she did work for a busy estate agency, lots of getting about meeting people, sometimes in empty houses, lots of male staff in the office, come to that. And thinking of that, how would she do her job from Bath if she intended to stay there? He could dream up all manner of opportunities – and even the motives – for infidelity, but somehow, they just weren't Phil.

Spurred by thinking about her job he sat up, reached for the phone and rang her office number. Then, thinking he was being silly, he put it down again before anyone answered.

He still loved her, he realised at that point. Somehow – but he didn't know exactly how – it would all be all right. Wouldn't it?

Then the doorbell rang. Tad.

They had the choice of two nearby pubs. They chose the Farmer's Boy, which was the furthest but usually quiet at that time of day, getting a drenching on the way over. In the small bar they bought beers – bitter for John and a Guinness for Tad – and sat at a vacant table, still in their wet coats like the eight or nine people already there, all men talking as if sharing secrets in the quiet local dialect. The thought crossed John's mind that the men were drinking to give themselves courage for the onslaught of Megastorm Miranda, as TV and radio reports were now calling it, making ready to leap up and take whatever action was necessary at a moment's notice. It gave the whole bar a damp, subdued atmosphere although it would have taken a very big wave indeed to reach this location.

"Well," Tad started, in the same low conspiratorial tone of the drinkers around them, "'ere we are." The square little Welshman, bald on top apart from a few greased strands combed back, winked. "A penny for them?"

John flicked back his own wet hair and took a deep draught. He had nothing to lose, he felt, by telling Tad his woes, so he did.

"I see," said Tad, when he had finished, "and you still really don't know why?"

"Could be a lot of things, I suppose," he said, then in an aggrieved voice added, "*and* it's a bloody company car!"

Tad thought for a moment, then said, "Tell you what – you won't be able to do anything about that problem until this storm thing's over, so it isn't worth trying. One more half, eh, and I'll come back home with you – got to anyway, I left my camera there. And then I'm heading for the office, if it's open, and then home for a kip. I've been up since bloody midnight, boyo. Why don't you do the same and I'll come by early tomorrow and pick you up and we'll go to Newnham to watch the crazy surfers. There's a story and a half cooking up there."

The proposition sort of made sense. At home, John said goodbye to his photographer-confidante, made himself a cup of tea, took it up to his bedroom and, shedding his wet trousers, put himself to bed. He shut his eyes, waiting for the tea to cool, but was asleep within minutes, the drink untouched. His sleep was a shallow, dream-ridden collage of unconnected images with the underlying theme of being pursued by an unidentifiable but assuredly deadly enemy.

***

Aside from the worsening flood threatening to enter from the Teme, the River Severn had problems of its own. It was overloaded almost to its source high in the land of boggy pools near the peak of Plynlimon, the vast high spongy dome dominating the centre of Wales from which the River Wye also sprang, perversely heading in the other direction, south. The Severn would once have had its own ways of dealing with excess rainwater if it hadn't been thwarted by the meddlesome human race. Once the growing torrent reached lower levels its 'normal' behaviour would be to flow over its banks into a gradually widening flood plain that wound almost all the way from Newtown (not too distant from the James' farm and the source of the Teme) all the way down to its tidal estuary. The land would have welcomed it, and the flooded grasslands – altogether a huge acreage – were a feature which annually welcomed thousands, if not millions, of overwintering waders, geese, Whooper and Bewick's swans from Russia and other birds escaping the harsh weather of more northerly latitudes. In spring, once February's rains had ceased, the land would have dried and a rich terrain of flower-strewn meadows, freshly supplied with nutrients, would re-emerge. Some such meadows survive today, locally known as 'hams', at the riverside in such places as Upton, Tewkesbury and Gloucester – because of their unique flora and fauna, many are protected Sites of Special Scientific Interest (SSSIs).

Gradually man has encroached on this former flood-plain and altered its natural mechanisms for dealing with winter deluges. Much land has been artificially drained with ditches and culverts, with every effort made to keep floodwater out by throwing up high banks. Housing estates and the infrastructure that surrounds them and links them, plus the expansion of industrial development, have all been designed to channel water back *into* the river rather than away from it.

Perhaps more subtly, man has been influencing weather patterns, largely through producing too much of the 'greenhouse effect' gas carbon dioxide. Temperatures in the biosphere are rising, the climate is changing. Storms and droughts alike are more frequent, more severe. Together with this series of whammies, today's predicted flooding in the upper Severn is already 'severe' according to Environment Agency warnings, and it will soon be collecting further trouble from the situation on the Teme, which it meets at Worcester.

In its wisdom, the Cobra committee along with Operation Sandbag had judged the river flooding threat alone to be so worrying that it ordered the evacuation of much of Upton-on-Severn and the entire old town area of Tewkesbury where, in a 2007 flood, only the famous 900-year-old abbey, built on a rise at the junction of the Severn and the Warwickshire Avon, plus the tops of a few tall buildings, were visible in a vast sea of water.

While the nation waited and watched fleets of buses were ferrying people from the Upton area eastwards towards safe high ground around the Malvern Hills, and from Tewkesbury towards the Cotswolds. Low-lying parts of Gloucester were also being evacuated after frantic sandbagging along the riverbanks below the old jail was deemed to be inadequate, futile. Hopefully its more elevated ancient and beautiful cathedral, the resting place of ill-fated Edward II and sometime set for *Harry Potter* films, would be safe.

The Environment Agency-led workforce were keeping a close watch on the career of the Teme's waterborne 'river monster' (as they were now calling it) which, by the time it had reached Ludlow, carried several tree-trunks, some rowing boats and a canoe, a crushed caravan, at least three wooden picnic tables and a newish Ford van. It was too dangerous to do much more than try to keep the mass on the move, rolling itself over and over, while downstream there was a concerted effort to move everybody and everything out of harm's way. As it passed below brooding Ludlow Castle – one of the first Norman stone castles to be built in England – it met a series of bank-to-bank weirs below the fortification's bluff. One of these, horseshoe-shaped, was of concern because it pinched the waterway and the 'monster' might have snagged, forming a formidable barrier, penning up water behind it. However, to the huge relief of the workforce and the growing gallery of townspeople who had gathered on the bluff and on the castle ramparts (where in spring many had stood to watch salmon trying to breast the weirs in a meagre flow) the rolling mass rumbled its way over all these restrictions with apparent ease. After it passed each obstruction it accelerated as it rolled on downstream, cheered on by the onlookers.

Bridges were another concern. There were many acts of heroism, mostly unrecorded, as men with boathooks eased the writhing branches under bridge arches while the masonry and ironwork underneath them shook in the flow, which was threatening to carry everything away, swollen as it was by more floodwater entering from the River Corv. Almost the entire town of Tenbury Wells turned out to watch it passing, and as the word got around that this was a once-in-a-lifetime spectacle, people started to line the banks ahead of it all the way to Worcester.

Yet to most of the workmen and their watchers in this part of the country this was simply a local problem. Megastorm Miranda, somewhere in the wings, was a media distraction, a distant threat that meant not a lot to them except that they might perhaps lose a few loose roof tiles.

Up in the Teme headwaters Owen and Alice James watched the unfolding drama on television. After hearing the appeal for people with hand-milking experience, Owen had volunteered his services to the NFU coordinator and had been asked to make himself available on standby 'just in case'. Owen had ample experience to back up his offer to help. In his Agricultural College holidays and for some time before he took the farm over from his father, he had been a 'relief milker' – on call to dairy farmers who wanted to give themselves or their dairy manager a break or if they fell ill. He remembered this with some affection. It had been a carefree life with very few responsibilities, just the morning and late afternoon milking, the rest of the time his own. He'd had a little grey Morris Minor estate car and if he used the time between his morning and afternoon duties to catch up on some sleep, he could indulge his evening passion for playing pub darts in a well-trodden circuit of the local hostelries. For drinks, of course. Woe betide any locals who thought him a novice, for he was hot as mustard on the doubles and trebles and rarely needed to pay for his beer! When he thought of his dairy duties now he could almost hear the steady *whoosh-whup* of the milking machinery and revisit the pleasant smell of the cows as they chewed patiently in their herringbone parlours, or lowed softly, waiting to be let out into their meadows again. Hand-milking was often a part of his work, especially if machinery broke down.

"We've had a lot of offers of mobile parlours," the NFU man said when Owen had telephoned, "But maybe not quite enough. If necessary, we can commandeer them directly from the manufacturers but in general everybody's being very helpful. Have you had experience of portable bails if we allocate you to one?"

"A bit. Well, actually, quite a lot – but do you know where I'm likely to be needed?"

There was a pause and a rustle of paper as if the man was consulting a list. Then he said: "Nothing your way – it's all quite clear. There's likely to be trouble lower down the Severn, though, and then there's Somerset, which we're really worried about, and areas like the Gwent Levels not far from Cardiff. Are you mobile?"

"Yes," he said, as he was put on the list. He looked at Alice.

"You can cope, can't you, if I have to go?"

He knew that she and Meg could manage very well.

***

Mervyn Connor and Michael Saunders had let both their organisations know they would not be home until the all-clear was called somewhere around teatime the next day, Thursday, or perhaps even longer than that. Both had been told they would probably have to stay one night at least in Portishead. Saunders was lucky that a change of clothing and some toiletries could be sent in to him from his home at Almondsbury, just to the north of Bristol. Connor was trying to arrange something similar, but suddenly Tavistock seemed to him to be a long way away. And there was nobody at home to tell all this to anyway, not since Mary had died two years ago. He wondered if he should call his daughter, Alice, in Norwich to find out if she was all right, but a little voice inside his head said 'of course she is', and he did not put this plan into action. Alice, a member of the climate pressure group Extinction Rebellion, would probably only say, "Well, we have been warning you. You should have known it was coming."

Connor and Saunders had reached a point where they thought Operation Sandbag had done all it could in advance of the actual storm, at least for the time being. On the table before the whole HQ group there was now a map showing the best and worst case extent of the flooding that could be expected. 'Definite' areas were marked out with a solid thick black line, and 'possible' extensions beyond that had a dotted border.

While the critical areas were mainly the Severn Vale, the West Country and parts of South Wales in particular, other points around Britain that looked particularly vulnerable to the coming exceptional high tide and its accompanying tidal surge had also been sketched in and allocated to six satellite areas with their own operational HQs. These were quickly up and running. Area One, based in Plymouth, covered the South Coast from Lizard Point all the way to Dover, and included The Solent with its particularly tricky double tide; Area Two covered the East Coast from Margate to Scarborough (including London of course), and Area Three butted into Scotland at Edinburgh. Area Four was most of the rest of the Scottish coast round to Glasgow, and Area Five ran on down to Liverpool. Area Six covered the coast of Wales round to Swansea. Ireland and Northern Ireland were making their own arrangements although, like the six satellite HQs, they were linked to Portishead so that aid could be directed towards any situation that needed it the most. In helping to set it all up

Connor had calculated as well as he was able the amounts of wind and rain and the intensity of the surge that could be directed at the country, while Saunders had drawn on the Environment Agency's records of past flooding to forecast possible scenarios.

"Actually, my head's spinning round and round now and I'm worried it might twist off altogether," Saunders had confided quietly to Carter after he had done the best he could to cover all the many areas of concern.

"Know what you mean. Shall we head out for a bit to clear our thoughts? A quick Italian, something like that. I've had nothing much to eat all day except coffee and cheese rolls."

Christine Lees, who had assumed the role of chairman and de facto 'boss' of the group, agreed to an hour off – so long as one of them at least covered for her for a break of her own when they came back.

"I don't think any of us is going to get any real sleep tonight, do you?" she said. It was a question that didn't need an answer. She added: "Park Street in the city's quite good for restaurants. I'll see if I can get you a lift."

The two men were driven in an unmarked police car to the rain-lashed centre of Bristol. Their eating place, recommended by the friendly young officer who drove them, went by the unlikely name of 'Moltobuono'. "My boyfriend takes me there sometimes," the neatly turned-out and smiley officer said. "The food's really nice. We call it 'The Montalbano.' The name sort of goes with police work!"

WPC Olivia Freeman dropped them off in a Strictly No Parking zone – "Just call it a company perk" – but declined an offer to join them for a meal, saying she had already eaten and she would get a coffee in a drive-through and drink it in the car, "You know, just like a real policeman! Anyway, you two must have a lot to talk over. I've only just come on duty, so I'd better go."

Inside the restaurant, there was a warm welcome but only two couples dining, plus a single man eating alone. A slow afternoon, then. Hardly surprising considering the weather. Still, the smells coming from the kitchen were appealing, and after seating them the waiter presented a menu, mainly pizzas and home-made pasta dishes. The latter seemed particularly appetising.

"Let's not," Saunders said suddenly after they had ordered two dishes and bottles of Italian beer. Connor arched an eyebrow.

"Let's not what?"

Saunders raised his beer and gave a conspiratorial wink. "Let's not talk about Miranda until we've finished enjoying this and had the usual argument about pudding."

Connor smiled, lifted his own beer. Momentarily, at least, it felt as if a weight had been lifted from his shoulders.

"Needed that," Connor said when they'd finished. "Now, I suppose, we really ought to consider plans. As I see it, I can't be much more use here. I need to be back in Exeter, in my bailiwick. I don't think our police boss realises that. If I stay here, I have to keep getting weather updates second-hand. Know what I mean? I'm going to make a bid for freedom."

Saunders nodded. "I see completely, although I'm fine where I am at Portishead. So long as the information keeps coming in, I can make a pretty good stab at probabilities as the situation develops. It would be handy, though, if we had some weather expertise on the spot. Is that a possibility?"

The restaurant door opened, and they turned to see their driver Olivia Freeman entering. She flashed a brief smile and gave them a little wave then seated herself at an empty table. The waiter immediately engaged her in conversation.

"Feels like we're about to be escorted off to the lock-up," said Connor. "Perhaps we should get back to it in a minute or two. What about me suggesting to our leader that I get a lift down to Exeter – it's no great distance down the M5 while it's still open – and then I'll send back two of my people in return. Would that work?"

Saunders nodded. Within the half hour, Connor was being driven swiftly south by Olivia Freeman. And ungallantly falling deeply asleep.

Chapter 12

That afternoon's high tide, peaking at just after 6pm, was fairly big, but far from the enormous threat to life or property that tomorrow morning's surge promised to be. Around the coast, the water climbed a long way up sea walls and threw itself over the top here and there, but most defences were shaken rather than stirred...

In entering river estuaries and tidal reaches its effect was more dramatic, for all rivers were swollen by the recent persistent rain. With the rising seawater stopping the outward flow or even, as in the Severn, pushing it back upstream, many of the earthwork walls built against 'normal' inundations were soon overtopped.

Places that were regularly flooded of course got an expected dose – people were used to that.

There was no travel along the main Gloucester-Cardiff train line down the Severn's west bank. Stretches of rail were completely submerged, and there were some doubts about the structural safety of the iron rail bridge near Gloucester, where acres of farmland had already turned into a spreading lake. Similarly, the A48 road from Gloucester was impassable at places like Minsterworth and the low land on the approach to Newnham, the traditional meeting spot for bore-riders.

***

"You'll do no such thing!"

The voice of the visiting Superintendent drafted in from Stroud was authoritative, and even the palm held up traffic-cop style would be forbidding enough to most people. But not to a doughty bore-rider, and especially not to a class one surfer in the Mad Jack Churchill tradition like wet-suited Alan Jenkins as, board under arm, he made his way to the water's edge. He gave the head officer a look that was almost a sneer.

"You can't stop me."

And before the Super realised Jenkins was in the water with a splash, throwing himself flat on the board, then paddling furiously with his hands in the direction of the Arlingham shore. Powerless and red-faced the Super watched as five more surfers followed him. Furious, he turned to the two local officers behind him.

"Why didn't you stop him … them?"

"What for?" asked one of them, trying hard to suppress a smirk.

"You know," said the Super, "we are supposed to stop them riding on this storm surge thing. It's for their own good, after all."

"But sir…"

"No 'buts'. This will go on your file. Both of your files."

"But sir," the officer said, realising the Super knew little about tides let alone bore-riding, "this isn't the storm surge or even the start of it. It's a big tide, but it will run back out quite quickly after going through. Quite safe to ride, I would think, specially for that lot. The surge is expected on the next high water."

"Oh? And when's that?"

The officer checked his watch.

"12 hours' time, near enough sir. That's around 6am tomorrow morning."

The Super stared at them both, then turned and made for his unmarked car while both the local policemen looked away, apparently studying a gathering of rowdy jackdaws on the roof of Unlawater House across the bend in the road, their shoulders shaking gently.

The Super climbed into the vehicle and was apparently overheard to say, "You people!" with some irritation before driving off.

The crowd that had gathered to watch the confrontation all turned with one accord to look down the broad river, where an approaching growl heralded the imminent arrival of the bore-before-the-big-one.

***

For seamen pitching and rolling in boats in the Western Approaches to land-dwellers in Ireland, Wales, and much of England and Northern France, there was widespread relief when the incessant heavy rain that had plagued their lives for days on end finally let-up a little. It did not stop entirely but settled back to a steady drizzle. Some even experienced a fleeting glimpse of a watery sun, filmy clouds scudding across its face. What most of the nation did not realise was that Miranda was merely taking a deep breath ahead of her grand tantrum.

Colin Roach knew better than to trust such a lull, however. He'd experienced something like this before before, and sure enough the moment he'd contacted *Anita* and promised his support in looking for two men in a dark and stormy sea, there were more thunderclaps and yet another buffeting squall, while the sky blackened to plunge them into semi-darkness. Stair-rod rain and more hail followed.

"We'd best get that net back in first," he said to Walby. "Come on."

Once again, the two men, one of them injured, fought their way to the stern of *Jocasta*, where the ropes securing the net that had stopped them pitching too steeply and going head-over-heels still streamed behind like a bridal train. In these conditions it would even have taken Superman several hours to draw in the wet netting by hand – hours that they did not have if they wanted to reach two men who even now might be dying of exposure.

"What now?" Walby said through gritted teeth, "We could cut 'un off."

But Roach thought if they got a rope secure on the net ropes beyond the otter boards and tied one end to the hydraulic winch drum, they could cut off the boards and winch the net in. It would save quite a bit of gear rather than throwing it overboard, although if cutting the net free had been what was required, he would have done it.

He fetched a length of rope from the port locker and, while Walby held onto his belt with one hand and the winch-frame with the other, he leaned forward over the water and made a passable knot. He then made a few turns round the winch spool with the free end of the rope. He pushed the winch control stick forward gently, holding onto the rope-end until the turns bit and the fastening taughtened. He signalled to Walby to hack through one net line after another with a filleting knife. The jury rig held. Roach then eased the winch into gear and the net came streaming back over the stern ramp while they exchanged brief smiles.

"Right," said the skipper, resolution returning to his face, "quick with the anchor now, then we're away."

Drenched but safely back in the wheelhouse they set-to hauling up the anchor, which fortunately had not snagged on anything and came away clean. Roach gunned the engine to keep their station until the next wave peak drove at them, taking *Jocasta* steeply up the slope until, at the crest, he could turn first broadside on – the most dangerous position for a boat in heavy seas – and then ride the forward edge of the deep trough that followed. Happily, not a lot of water slopped over her freeboard and if he hadn't been so busy Roach would have taken some pride from the manoeuvre. As it was, he knew they would soon be at the bottom of the trough and the next wave would catch up with them. With full power he could ride the wave for some distance before the peak overtook them and the whole process started again.

He hated strong following seas, especially malevolent ones like this. In the troughs it felt as if they were in a deep, deep valley of black water from which they would never emerge. The waves coming up on them from behind looked like insurmountable mountains, the crests hanging over them until, at the last minute, *Jocasta* lifted her stern and was propelled forward as if by an invisible hand. If any of these waves had broken over the stern *Jocasta* would surely have been swamped. Even if a swamping only disabled them slightly they would be at the complete mercy of the next wave crashing on top of them, ton upon ton of falling water – just the situation that many mariners saw seconds before drawing their last breath...

Roach asked Walby to check on their seasick invalid. If all was well, he could take the port lookout while he himself scanned to starboard.

"Boy's all right," Walby reported minutes later. "Breathing good. Don't think anything will wake him."

"Is he warm enough?" asked Roach without turning, gripping the wheel and screwing his eyes up to peer forward through the weather.

"Oh aye, I reckon. Proper job. Be nice if we could be tucked up in our beds now, wouldn't it?"

"And your finger, how is it?"

"I'll live, 'opefully."

After almost half an hour Roach was about to say to his crewman that he thought their task was a hopeless one, but then he saw a smudge of something orange far ahead in the gloom before they sank into yet another deep black trough.

"What was it?" asked Walby, tensing.

"Don't know. Could have been a container – bit of one, anyway. I'll take us nearer if I can. Keep your eyes skinned when we reach the next peak."

"There, look!"

Walby was pointing, excited. They were indeed coming up fast on a pyramid of orange metal that was sometimes sticking out of a boiling sea then plunging back under again. Roach turned his wheel as far as he thought safe to get them closer, which took all his concentration, while Walby scanned the nearby water for signs of life.

"Nothing, not here. But there may be more containers ahead?"

Roach swung to starboard to keep well clear of the gyrating object in case it went under again and resurfaced under *Jocasta*'s hull, which would have meant the end of the rescue operation, and probably the end of them too. Rescue, that was, if there were any men still alive. Had anyone tried hanging onto this container they would have quickly drowned. Safely skirting the hazard, he caught the next wave crest and they surged forward again, hoping they might get another sighting. There was nothing for about a quarter of a mile but then they struck lucky – not one but two more objects ahead. As they closed in, they saw two containers about twenty yards apart, the nearest bobbing in and out of the surface like the one they had just left, but the furthest one about three quarters-submerged, end uppermost. And there was something on it!

"Get some ropes ready. And the lifebuoy."

"Dreckly!"

Walby, despite his injury, was already on the case, moving around the heaving deck to take a coil of nylon rope out of a locker and then unhitching the lifebuoy on the cabin's outside wall. He secured one end of the rope to a deck stanchion, and did the same with the lifebuoy rope. However, until they got closer it was still impossible to make out clearly if the objects were indeed men. With the engine on full ahead to keep abreast, Roach steered *Jocasta* in again. At the top of a wave which allowed him to look down on the container, Walby reported they were looking at first one, then two men trying to hang on like limpets. Bracing himself against the low gunwale, he weighed a coil of the rope in his good hand. He would be able to throw it as much as seven or eight yards in good conditions, but in this weather … and he'd only get one shot at it, maybe two.

"One alive at least. Waving."

Not much of a wave though. The other man looked lifeless.

"Tell them to catch it and tie themselves on!" Roach yelled. "Hope they understand English. Filipino, their skipper said. *Kurbata Sa*, I think, means 'hang on' – sailed with some once or twice."

"Tie on! Kurbata sa!" Walby screamed into the wind. To make sure the message got across he clutched the coil between his knees to free both hands and make a dumb show of tying a rope about himself, under his armpits, then holding on tight so that he could be hauled to safety.

"Coming in now!"

He picked up the coil again. *Jocasta* lurched closer on the crest of a wave, and it seemed almost as if they were going to roll right on top of the container and the men, but he got a line right across the two bodies just as the fishing boat rolled upright again. It then rolled the other way. Walby had to wait until they once again came upright from the wallow to see that the conscious man was tying the rope around his companion's chest, not his own. Walby hoped the man was alive.

He had no idea if he would be able to get another line over after the first rescue, if God allowed them to bring the first man back safely, but even as this thought crossed his mind the man was pushing his companion over the side of their makeshift refuge, bracing his back on the container and using both feet to shove. As he splashed into the water his companion quickly followed him, held on to the rope and started to kick out towards *Jocasta* while Walby bellowed "Help! Now!" to bring Roach out of the wheelhouse to assist.

Roach's immediate move was to drop the lifebuoy ahead of the swimming man, hoping he had strength enough to hold on while they hauled his companion out. The swimmer got the message and grabbed it. While *Jocasta* trundled along with nobody at the spinning wheel Roach held onto Walby while he reached down to catch hold of one man, and after him the second. Eventually they had both men on the deck, then manhandled them into the cabin between them.

A container-load of fashionable Brazilian shoes, minus its passengers, bobbed swiftly on towards England's westward shores.

The rescued men were safe for now, but one was in a pretty bad way – hypothermia, Roach guessed – and his companion wasn't much better. They put them on the padded cushions opposite the still-sleeping Jago Nancarrow, covered them with all the blankets and coats they could find, and Roach took the wheel again to bring *Jocasta* as gently as he could round to face into the weather again.

"What now?" Walby spoke tersely.

"We need to get them into port as quick as we can," said Roach, "so we make a course for Newlyn, I guess. I'll radio *Anita* and everyone we've picked them up – they'll be glad of that. Perhaps we can rendezvous with the Penlee lifeboat on the way. They'll know best what to do. We may not be able to get into Newlyn if the weather worsens so we've got a pretty uncomfortable night ahead, all in all. What do you think?"

Walby said he thought the plan was risky but perhaps the only one possible. They were still a long way from being home and dry. But he was glad they'd made a successful rescue. What they needed now was to stay alert and awake, and have the skill to ride the bad weather, which was now wild and getting wilder by the minute.

While Roach made his radio calls, young Jago woke and sat up suddenly, alert and apparently no longer suffering from *mal de mare*.

"What's up?" he said. "Where are we? And who are those?"

He was looking at the two apparently lifeless bodies on the seats opposite.

"Them?" Walby teased, glad to see they had another apparently fit spare hand. "Oh, *them* you mean. They're mermaids, they are, caught fresh while you were having your little nap."

Chapter 13

Exeter was keeping an anxious eye on its flood defences while the evening tide peaked. Upstream the River Exe had already gone over in a few 'hot spots' where flooding could often be expected, but it was the seaward banking and lagoon-like water-retaining ponds that gave everyone the most worry, and the relatively new works along the estuary down to Exmouth in particular.

Exeter had a long history of flooding recorded since the Middle Ages. Before newer works much of the banking had been built following disastrous floods in the 1960s and 70s, when more than 1,000 properties were inundated. The multi-million 2018-19 scheme was designed to protect some 3,000 additional properties from more serious events. However, even as it was completed the Environment Agency was predicting it could not fully protect everyone from an extreme event like the one that now threatened the town.

When Mervyn Connor and Olivia Freeman reached the Met Office's HQ he sent someone to bring the driver coffee and something to eat and left her in his office while he started to read the incoming data, moving around his staff and their monitors. Like the crewmen on *Jocasta* he knew he faced the prospect of a long and sleepless 24 hours, possibly more, even though he'd already been going since the wee small hours except for a few snatches of sleep while he was driven down the M5.

The situation was not good: if anything, things seemed to be getting worse. He went to the window to think, looking out on a gloomy scene.

It had passed changeover time for shifts, but a lot of people were still at their stations, sensing they might be needed. That was good, but some of them had to be released. Connor knew that back at Portishead, Saunders had asked for some Met Office assistance – intermediaries to feed him jargon-free data relayed from Exeter. It occurred to him that Caroline Cleaver and Mike Winter had been reading the situation from the start and they might be the ideal choice. So, some staff had to stay, some had to go home, and two had to go to Portishead, back up the M5 with Olivia Freeman if she'd been sufficiently rested. After taking care of the away-team he mentally picked his stayers, aware he'd have to get them to clear things with their families, and then turned to setting it all in motion.

"They said it was urgent, sir."

Connor was briefing Caroline Cleaver for her new role at Bristol when somebody handed him a printed message. Breaking off to read it, his face became serious.

"More trouble?" Caroline raised her eyebrows.

"Mm. Could be. It's a request for me and Saunders to get our heads together to predict if a situation like this is ever likely to repeat itself. As if we haven't got enough on our plates."

"Is it important right now?"

"I'm afraid so. It's via Miss Mastermind from the Prime Minister, so it's a three-line whip. But I don't think she'll really like what we're going to have to tell her."

Connor had no idea how well the Prime Minister had been briefed on the probable effects of climate change, but he had little doubt the impending surge riding on the wings of a massive storm was more than likely to have been spawned by the unprecedented – and accelerating – human-induced changes in world weather patterns.

It wasn't as if nobody had been warned that disaster was waiting around the corner. There were climate-change sceptics, who dismissed all talk of man-made weather changes as 'normal' wobbles that could be ignored (and some people even thought the earth was flat), but by and large every sane person as well as the climate activist Greta Thunberg had a fair idea that Britain, and indeed the rest of the world, was up against it, and mightily so.

The major culprit in all this was 'greenhouse gas', principally carbon dioxide generated by the burning of fossil fuels like coal and oil, which had formed a blanket in the upper atmosphere. This was dramatically raising the earth's temperature by trapping heat and not allowing it to radiate harmlessly away into space.

Every degree the temperature was raised by had a profound effect world-wide. Warmer sea temperatures drove animals and plants that could only live in cooler water further south and north. The warmer air melted polar icecaps and glaciers to release water that could ultimately raise sea levels by as much as two metres, threatening coastal communities and even covering low-lying presently populated islands. What was more, warmer seas generated more little twirly-whirly wind-devil squalls that grew and grew as they crossed tropical seas, reaching landfall as hurricanes and tropical cyclones and driving further and further and more fiercely inland. Being warm meant they picked up more moisture too, dumping it as rain in huge amounts, often where it was not wanted. New weather-related problems were also being reported: prolonged (and hotter) droughts, major bush fires in baked-dry forests and heaths and, oddly, big snowfalls where it had rarely snowed before. In short, the old 'reliable' weather patterns were going haywire…

Hitherto unheard-of side effects were also beginning to show themselves. The big, deep oceans could no longer hold the amounts of oxygen they used to carry, becoming barren for plant and fish life, and coral reefs with their associated bountiful life were dying as carbon dioxide made the seas more acidic. Much of Europe and North America had suffered the hottest summer temperatures ever recorded, with several fatalities.

Connor and Saunders, naturally, knew all this. They also knew that the number and frequency of disastrous weather events was increasing. Another degree in all likelihood meant bigger, more intense and more frequent storms, including hurricanes and tropical cyclones, delivering higher wind speeds and more rain and hail. There would be more storm surges of 20 feet or more on shores almost anywhere, pushed on by hurricane-force winds. There would be more severe flooding, more heatwaves, more wildfires, more severe droughts. It appeared unstoppable and was perhaps even an existential threat to human life – unless some drastic, earth-embracing action was taken, and taken quickly. Provided it was not already too late…

Perhaps unsurprisingly, some countries that had the most reliance on fossil fuels were holding out against carbon-cutting agreements. That reserves of oil and coal still in the ground or under the sea might be finite did not for the moment concentrate their minds on looking for alternatives such as, say, creating solar energy schemes in warmer climes or backing electricity storage research.

A frustrating impasse held sway while this relatively small and extremely fragile planet hurtled towards…what? Oblivion quite possibly.

***

At 10pm, with the tide falling away, many people in Britain could be forgiven for thinking there wasn't all that much to worry about. The rivers were high, sure – that had happened before in their memories with only local effects. Likewise, they had experienced storm warnings which in the end turned out to affect very few lives.

Journalist John Carter woke, at once fully alert, just as the last of the feeble daylight was leaving the room. He padded over to the telephone – but nobody had called, no word from his wife. Unsure about exactly what he was going to do next, he found dry clothes and shoes, put them on and went out into their tiny grassed back garden. He looked up. There was an odd sort of sky, the heavy clouds a dark grey-pink, strangely luminous and uniform from horizon to horizon. It was still raining, though not so heavily as it had done in the day, more like handfuls of water thrown petulantly every now and then. At first, he hadn't noticed the wind, but then from a long way off he heard a long, deep sough whistling through the treetops towards him. It rudely buffeted shrubs and rattled windows as it struck, and then moved on, abating, while the approach of another sough was growing behind it. Was this the approach of Megastorm Miranda?

***

Much the same thought was crossing Mervyn Connor's mind as he looked through his office windows. She was out there, Miranda, gathering all her forces, and she would soon be bringing a load of trouble to the party.

***

Owen and Alice James were keeping an eye on their television, as indeed most Britons were. While some of the commercial channels were continuing with their advertised entertainment programmes, the main ones were now given over entirely to rolling Miranda news mixed with travel warnings and flood prevention advice.

"I can't see it's going to affect us all that much up here, can you?" Alice asked her husband as they were shown yet more file shots of huge waves crashing against breakwaters, people overtaken by lashing seaside spray, cars being carried along swollen rivers and overwhelmed houses crumbling then tumbling into raging watercourses.

"No," Owen agreed, then added thoughtfully: "But it's going to be a grim old night for many, isn't it? And I wonder what's happening with all that muck and water that went down the river from here? That's bound to be a big headache for some."

His wife shrugged.

"Nothing we can do now. We'll just have to wait and see."

***

Cais felt a huge weight lift off his shoulders when he heard of the rescue of his two missing crewmen, although he knew they had a long way to go before they were safely landed. His new course took *Anita* almost directly into the weather, but he found that his new configuration, heeled to one side and with just one really fully effective screw, made him veer off to port across the rising wind if he ran the engine at full steam. Half-power was considerably slower, but it kept the other screw mostly in the water, which allowed him to maintain steerage and keep on course. All he could hope for now was that the weather did not worsen much more, and that by the time they reached safe anchorage things would have quietened down.

He was worried about the missing containers, and indeed feared they might lose more. And perhaps his seamanship would later be called into question by his bosses, although in the matter of financial damage the insurers would bear the brunt of his losses. Was it now time for him to quit and take a comfortable retirement? He was the right age for that, and his wife and children (although mostly grown up now) would be pleased.

The salvage tug *Afon Wen* might well rendezvous at some point ahead if they were making good progress. Should he take their offer of help? Costly for someone, but no skin off his nose. But it would be his decision. Better perhaps to wait and see what sort of condition *Anita* was in by the time they met and decide then.

A sudden lurch interrupted his thoughts. It felt briefly as if the whole ship had been lifted, raised into the stormy heavens, and he could now hear a redoubled scream of wind coming from the superstructure outside. He waited for her to come crashing down again. But she did not, and neither was she flying – the sea had almost miraculously flattened, stopped its runs of peaks and deep troughs, and looked instead as if it was boiling, seething beneath *Anita*'s hull. And she rode on steadily now, as if grateful for more straightforward going, but something more fundamental seemed to have happened for her forward speed had dropped by five knots. Cais had heard old sailors talk of such a phenomenon but had never experienced it himself – it felt as if his ship was plugging *uphill*.

***

Jocasta too rose on the boost of water, tucking her stern up high. And in the increasing gale she rode like a surfboard towards Cornwall and safety. Colin Roach was forced to take his fishing boat's speed up four knots to keep steerage and stop slewing sideways. On this flat but seething mass of water *Jocasta* was moving as fast as she had ever done. At least there were no longer any chasing peaks to overwhelm them from behind.

Roach exchanged messages with the Penlee lifeboat as it passed them unseen about a mile to the east.

"All well. Won't risk transfer – heading for Newlyn. Good luck with *Anita*."

"Thank you, *Jocasta*. Good luck to you too."

***

Anyone near seashores and river mouths that evening watched the tide pull out as far as anyone could ever remember. At Aberystwyth on the Welsh west coast a vast underwater forest of petrified tree stumps appeared. Divers had noted the underwater curiosities a few times before but now anyone who wanted to brave a growing wind and lashing sleety rain could inspect them at close hand on foot.

At Kennack Sands on Cornwall's Lizard Peninsula a dog-walker braving the storm swore he saw the ghostly shape of a near-complete three-masted wooden vessel lying high and dry on the greatly enlarged, newly scooped-out beach. Wrecked treasure ships, particularly those bearing pirate hoards, were much rumoured in this area, so for the time being he sat on his findings and vowed to return and see what loot might lie within it.

In Morecambe Bay, renowned for its vast low-tide flats and notorious for the drowning of 24 immigrant cockle-pickers who were overtaken by an incoming tide in the early 2000s, it did not look as if there was any sea at all, even if you should walk to the horizon beyond the offshore wind farm...

And from Land's End to the Mull of Galloway, people were puzzling over the disappearance of the entire West Coast's seagulls, normally plentiful and particularly pesky in seaside-holiday towns and villages. There were many reports of hundreds of them wheeling together in great, noisy flocks before vanishing in a body inland. Did they know something that people did not?

Beside the lower tidal River Severn at Newnham, surfboarder Alan Jenkins had showered and dressed after getting a lift back from Minsterworth, where the afternoon tide had taken him. He stood by the carpark and viewpoint and looked out across the broad riverbed. It was almost dry now, apart from a fifteen-foot wide channel of angry brown water carrying God knows what rubbish running fast towards the Arlingham side. In normal times such a flow would be a tame affair, and it would be easy for anyone to walk right across the estuary, bank to bank.

It had not been his best ride, he admitted to himself. The wave had not stood up well, being cancelled to a large extent by the sheer amount of floodwater coming down the river, and only the experienced riders like him (two at the end in fact) had been able to 'read' all its nuances well enough to stay aloft. What was more, the exposed river bed was now dotted with some of the snags he'd had to dodge on the way – several tree-stumps, a pub's picnic table, beer kegs and oil and rain barrels, endless plastic bottles, a scattering of dead spent salmon. What would tomorrow's monster really be like? He had no idea. Shrugging, he turned his back on it all and walked home to finish rinsing the sand and mud out of his wetsuit and snatch some sleep in readiness for braving the wild waters of the morning.

***

John Carter at last got a mobile call from his wife. Phyllis was in Mitcheldean, on the far side of Cinderford. So, she hadn't gone all that far.

"Are you stranded?" he asked, shaking off a fuzzy head from sleeping at an unaccustomed hour after a few beers.

So far as she knew, not – but there had been all sorts of warnings on the radio and boards beside the roads about the flooding round Gloucester and there was already lots of standing water on the surfaces, so she hadn't pressed on. She was now with an old riding friend, Jane.

"Are you coming back?"

"Jane says I can stay tonight. Tomorrow I might come back. Or I can leave the car here, go on by bus. I know you need it and I'm sorry I took it. I just had to go."

"I can change things. We can talk. We can sort it out."

Pause.

"I'll call you tomorrow."

She switched off her phone.

Chapter 14

Ireland got it first. Miranda's approach began with sudden powerful and practically unannounced mountain of water crashing against the islets and heads and surging up the deep inlets of the South, racing at express speed up to Tralee, pouring into Dingle Bay and the Kenmare River, Bantry Bay and the aptly-named Roaringwater Bay, scattering and sinking boats and driving some ashore, flooding homes, carrying off unwisely-parked vehicles and holiday caravans, and drowning three people at different locations who had unwisely come to the shore to watch her arrival. It wasn't as if nobody had been warned, and nor was this event entirely unprecedented. In January 2018 Storm Eleanor had given this part of the world a real thrashing, while a year earlier, in mid-October, Hurricane – yes, *Hurricane* – Ophelia had sprung from nowhere in the Azores to batter the entire country, again claiming the same number of deaths – three people – in the Emerald Isle.

Tonight, the authorities had predicted, would be worse, and so it was. The screaming wind that accompanied the wild water was strengthening by the minute. The power grids that served Tralee, Killarney, Kenmare and Skibbereen went down, leaving thousands of homes and businesses without electricity and further hampering recue efforts in dark and flooded streets. Clonakilty, Kinsale and Cork towns were bracing themselves for the worst. Shannon and Cork airports had been shut down, and at Donegal, Dublin and Belfast flights were severely restricted. If anyone slept through the fierce storm's arrival and eventual departure on the entire island, they were lucky indeed.

Miranda moved on.

She took an almost-affectionate little taster, a nibble and a lick at the offshore rocky reefs and sands surrounding the high and dry impregnable-looking bastion of far South West Britain, and toyed with the little scattered Isles of Scilly archipelago, in better times hailed as "the Maldives of the Atlantic" and cut off now because their main means of getting to and from the mainland, the aging ferry *The Scillonian* and a superannuated helicopter, had been stood down as inoperable in such conditions.

The Scillies were reasonably lucky this time. By now Miranda had hunched her muscular shoulders up like a burly rugby prop, and the hurricane was driving this massive black hump rapidly past the five inhabited islands, just missing them, and heading its main bulk straight at North Cornwall. Instead of the battering they had feared the inhabitants of the low-lying islands lost several acres from their sand dunes while the water went on rising to the highest levels ever recorded and homes and businesses were inundated. At St Mary's, flood prevention boards and sandbags were swept away as the swell topped 30ft (previously Eleanor had presented them with a swell of 29.9ft). And annoyingly, the water did not show any signs of receding any time soon. The ferocious wind that had come with it raged on. However, the islands hadn't been smashed or entirely inundated as some had feared. But apparent salvation from the main brunt of the storm did not make the inhabitants less anxious for the more distant future – so vulnerable are the Scillies to extreme weather that there is talk of the archipelago being entirely abandoned should global warming produce some of the rising sea levels being predicted.

As if impatient with holding back, Miranda suddenly lost all her coyness and dropped the deceptive foreplay. The fury that struck Cornwall was roaring, ruthless and abandoned, like a wanton drunkard throwing crunching blows everywhere, determined to bowl down anyone and anything in the way.

Well inland, people said afterwards, you could feel a judder through the ground as the first of a series of big waves struck the rocky Land's End peninsula, and you could hear a whoosh, boom and a roar as the water towered up and spray was hurled over the heads and clifftops. It was as if the whole country was shaking.

As predicted, while the main mass of angry water moved northwards, the still-rising sea behind it divided at Sennen and one part of the torrent pushed rapidly east into Mounts Bay, flooding into Newlyn, Penzance and Porthleven before rounding Lizard Point, heading into the Helston River and Falmouth, and racing on and on to the English Channel.

The monster heading north-north east, however, was really the storm that nobody wanted. It smashed into St Ives Bay in the growing light of early dawn, sweeping away the long sands beneath the neat rows of yachts and fishing boats in Carbis Bay swinging, as marine safety advised, on long chains with snubbers – weak links of stretchy rope or more fancy coiled metal springs – to dampen the snatch as the anchor line tightened at the top of each wave. Not all boats held fast. Many broke away to ride the roiling water up on to the beach, or past the the protective stone barricades of the harbour and on to the suddenly very vulnerable-looking harbour-edge pubs, restaurants and shops. Initially many people could be forgiven for thinking that Miranda's first resounding slap against the harbour roadside was the worst she could do ... but then the water rose and kept on rising, topping the wall, pushing on into homes and businesses while villagers fought in the screaming wind to salvage what they could.

It was, they said, Eleanor with knobs on. The January storm of 2018 had also topped the wall, destroying among other things an art gallery and its valuable paintings, but Miranda pushed on in far faster and deeper than that. And even later, when the tide would normally have started to ebb, the overall water level remained stubbornly high, a sort of "you're not done with me yet" defiance.

The ever-rising water and its reluctance to clear quickly was to continue to be the case as Miranda's assault went on and on up the north Cornish coast and beyond: Portreath, St Agnes, Perranporth (where half the Penhale Sands had disappeared when the water at last went down), Newquay (Fistral beach lost decking and businesses were badly damaged), around St Agnes Head and up to Padstow at the head of the long Camel estuary, Tintagel, Bude, and on and on…

It wasn't as if the folk in these seaside communities (or indeed those further inland) had nothing else to worry about. Like the rest of the country they had already suffered days and days of almost incessant rain. The normally placid streams and rivers running off the moors and high ground were best described as raging torrents. Many people had already moved out of vulnerable properties, fearing the flash-flood fate and resultant loss of lives that had befallen Linton, Lynmouth and Boscastle within living memory.

By and large, however, people were well prepared, even if they hadn't fully grasped the magnitude of 'megasurge' Miranda's savagery. The Met Office and the Environment Agency between them had made a good job of their forecasting, as far as they were able, and the rescue services were swinging into action. Thus, when Miranda swept into the broad Taw and Torridge estuary and up to Bideford and Barnstable, whole areas of housing had been safely evacuated and quays and bridges and riverside roads were closed and abandoned to their fate. As predicted a vast inland lagoon of sea and muddy river water began to form, which grew and grew.

At Linton on most clear days it's easy to see some of Swansea's buildings and oil refineries across the Severn, which is very wide at this point. At night too you can see the ruddy flare-offs at the tops of refinery chimney stacks. However, this stormy morning, with the ragged and racing deep grey clouds seemingly just above the headlands, nobody who had retreated well up the steep road from the harbour could see very much at all – save that much of the lower village was covered up by the sea with one lick, as it were, jetty, pubs, boats, houses and all. The buildings re-emerged when the wave drew back, much to everyone's relief, but this was tempered by disappointment when the seething water settled at first floor level for many properties and looked determined to stay there for the time being.

Linton is a significant spot for Miranda: from here on in the estuary begins to narrow, and local boatmen will tell you the effect of this makes the tides fickle, less than predictable. Water cannot be compressed. It has to overcome confinement. Has to.

***

Monitoring satellite weather images had been Exeter's main duty through the long night, and they were relaying the most significant these on to Cleaver and Winter at the Operation Sandbag nerve-centre in Portishead, along with updated forecasts and suggestions about measures that might be necessary to prevent loss of life and limb. Among these, it had been decided to close the M5 motorway to all traffic from the start of the Levels at the foot of the Mendips south of Bristol all the way down to the Bridgwater exit. Indeed, on motorways everywhere it had been recommended that truckers halt runs for 48 hours, more because of the expected wind-buffeting high-sided vehicles were likely to take than because of flooding. Traffic, though light, was already beginning to back up on the M5 through Bristol as well as along the M4 and M48 leading into the city. Because of this Portishead itself was beginning to feel isolated, its road access blocked.

Ever since Miranda had reached the Irish coast the storm had come more and more to resemble a picture of the sort of huge revolving weather systems brewed in mid-Atlantic, the ones that more frequently these days battered America after trailing death and destruction through the Caribbean. To Mervyn Connor in Exeter, and indeed to many others, she had also become a personality, at times predictable, at times surprisingly capricious, but always bearing a lurking sense of menace. Currently her offshore wind speeds had tipped an incredible 75mph (winds must hit 64 knots, 118kmh or 74mph to be considered hurricane force).

Connor's latest prediction was that Miranda's destructive outer edge would hit the Somerset coast square-on at about high tide – now just a matter of minutes away – and once she had made landfall she would turn sharply north-eastwards and rapidly weaken to a severe rain depression, her remnants then heading off to Scandinavia. She would become less potent because she would no longer be drawing up moisture from the Gulf Stream-warmed sea, an essential condition for Atlantic hurricanes. This would starve the convection system currently spiralling humid air into the upper atmosphere. But there were other matters on his mind – he was trying to explain the mechanics of a 'seiche' to a group of colleagues. He was standing, and the six other people were mostly leaning against the walls except for Marion Cooper (aka Miss Mastermind) who had swung rank and taken his seat. He'd turned his monitor so that everyone could see the series of smooth wavy lines crossing left-right across the screen.

"Normal peak-trough wave pattern. But when you get this situation on water …"

He tapped his keyboard to introduce a far slower wave that rolled continually back and forth, left, right, right, left, as if rebounding from each side.

"That's the pattern of a seiche, which occurs when a strong wind or some other factor drives large bodies of enclosed or semi-enclosed water against one shore, tilting the plane of the whole surface first one way then back towards the other. While the water lingers against one or the other shore it pushes up a standing wave that can persist for some time, otherwise known as a seiche. I think we're just about to get one now in the Severn Estuary. In fact, I believe we've hit just about the conditions that caused the monumental disaster people called the great flood of 1607 – a standing wave riding ashore on a high tide and storm surge driven by hurricane-force winds. In pretty much the same place too. There's no time to do anything more about it than we've already done, and despite the fact we're streets ahead of the forecasting abilities of the Seventeenth Century, I fear things could be a good deal worse than we imagine. I hope – I pray - I'm wrong."

There was silence, during which Connor switched his monitor back to the EN.SAT24 real-time images of Miranda's cartwheeling progress.

Marion Cooper was the first to speak.

"You've told all this to our people in Portishead?"

It was the first time Connor had seen her worried like this. Of course there would be repercussions for them all, but her especially, if the forecasting was in any way inaccurate. But then they didn't actually *make* the weather, did they?

"They're as ready as they can be," he said, adding with a nod at the swirling hyperactive image on his screen, "and here she comes."

Chapter 15

The Penlee lifeboat turned back when it was radioed that *Anita* had come through the worst of the storm and was making steady, if slow, progress towards Cork with her remaining crew safe and well. The wind had dropped, the swell was settling to a steadier roll and visibility had improved considerably now that the fret had gone, and the dawn light was growing. Nevertheless, both *Afon Wen* and the Navy oiler were shadowing the cargo ship in case they were needed. Cais did not think he would be needing their services now. If he could get his containers rearranged and secured, he could continue his journey with a lot of the goods he started out with intact. His reception back in his home port might not be quite so bad as he had feared.

The lifeboat skipper had now decided to trail *Jocasta* in as a bit of insurance for the fishing boat and her rescued container ship crewmen. For them too the weather was starting to let up a bit, which was a huge relief. The reports from Newlyn, however, were not that good. The flooding they had experienced beat anything served up in recent years. Both the lifeboat and *Jocasta* would need to hold off for some time until the onshore hoo-hah had died down and there was a chance of safe anchorage. There were lots of loose boats of all shapes and sizes about too, they learned, both in and out of the harbour, adding to the danger of unpredictable currents.

***

A long way up-country in Worcestershire, as soon as the Teme's pent-up floodwater had reached the river mouth at Worcester, it had met the Severn's own considerably swollen flow, which was already forcing its way into riverside homes and town businesses.

Up to this point the Severn flooding had been reasonably predictable, with much more time to prepare for certain overtopping from Shrewsbury, down through Bridgnorth, Bewdley and Stourport and on to Worcester. Below the town it was a different matter – the combined flows of both the rivers Teme and Severn, with mountains of floating debris, did not bode well for the bankside settlements that lay ahead. Upton-on-Severn had been all but abandoned, which was just as well, for the broad flood-plain hams became enormous lakes in a matter of minutes.

Hardly an Upton building was untouched by the muddy assault, and it was the same picture all the way down to Tewkesbury and the Severn's confluence with the also-flooded Shropshire Avon, Shakespeare's river, with the debris acting like a moving dam and helping to spread the swollen waters far and wide. Pleasure boats that had lined the river banks bobbed off their long mooring poles, many compressed into untidy jumbles against hedges along with bankside mobile holiday homes and caravans, or joined the moving stream of debris – a re-run of 2007, the wettest summer since records began in 1776. Back in 2007 Tewkesbury's old town had been completely cut off with the army drafted in to help in the relief effort. Aerial pictures showing water lapping at the fringes of the ancient abbey and completely submerging the main streets beyond are unforgettable images of the disaster, which claimed three lives. The flooding then left 48,000 homes without power for several days and fresh water had to be trucked in by the Army.

This time, with only a few hours left before a high tide and dire warnings of an impending storm surge, the lights of Tewkesbury went out again, and the water rose and rose...

After learning its lesson in 2007, and again to a lesser extent in 2017 when there was also widespread flooding, the town that was normally the furthest point reached by Severn tidal water had been more or less completely evacuated, with its historic buildings heavily sandbagged. It's said that some clergy at the abbey had booked themselves a grandstand view of the proceedings, looking down at the disaster from the massive square tower's parapets.

***

At 5.50am precisely Miranda's tidal surge rippled along Bridgwater Bay's north-facing coast at an enormous pace, licking high up the cliff bulwarks to the snaking coastal path above, and biting into anchorages at Porlock, Minehead and Watchet, at the seaward end of the Quantock Hills. Past Quantoxhead, with spray flying high into the air, it surged around the heavily shored-up Hinkley Point nuclear stations, overran the Steart peninsula and the marshes it sheltered and then slammed into Burnham-on-Sea as if it had been saving all its wrath for the occasion. The sea wall gave way almost immediately, washed away like a child's sandcastle. The surge had now reached the soft underbelly of a vast area of low-lying farmland known as the Somerset Levels – an area laced with drainage channels stretching north from Bridgwater, north to the foothills of the Mendips under Wells (including Glastonbury and its famous Tor) and past Cheddar and east to Somerton, all the way up to Weston-Super-Mare.

It announced its arrival with a screaming wind and driving, almost-horizontal rain, immediately overwhelming the barrages and storm banks that had been reinforced since the 2013-14 floods that had inundated 64 square kilometres of normally peaceful grazing land and withy and reed beds. It mattered not that the main inland watercourses, like the rivers Brue and Parrett and the King's Sedgemoor Drain, had been deep-dredged since the last disaster to allow them to offer more capacity and hopefully take away any more flooding quickly. There was far too much water for this to have any effect this time.

Many who had the dubious benefit of being able to watch the tidal surge's progress overland – people on higher spots such as Glastonbury Tor – were astonished by its rapid advance. Rather than swallowing everything with a huge wave, the water seemed to come from the bottom up, and almost everywhere at once: fields in an instant became waterlogged, with just the tips of grass and crops showing, and then minutes later they were swallowed altogether, drowned in a vast and still-rising sea-water lake running to the distance in every direction and broken only by a few tree-tops and mini-islands. Long stretches of the M5 motorway were quickly submerged.

Having overrun coastal defences to cover this vast area with an action not unlike water slopping over the rim of an over-filled bowl, the surge now swirled across to the west bank of the wide estuary and found easy ingress to low-lying land from Swansea up to Cardiff bay and into Cardiff, on to the Gwent Levels up to Chepstow and the Lancaut Peninsula at the mouth of the River Wye, and on and on ... and not levelling or falling back once it had overtopped these areas, but continuing to rise as more and more water pushed in from behind. When it eventually reached its peak, it was in some areas a good 20ft above any flooding encountered in living memory – a good 25ft above sea level.

Now it had reached the gradually narrowing river mouth, a toothpaste-tube effect driving up a massive bore wave pushing steadily towards the downward-speeding flood water and flotsam in the Severn.

Almost as soon as the water had topped the hedges in the Levels on both sides of the estuary, small rescue boats – particularly the Severn Area Rescue Association rubber dinghy lifeboat fleet – set out in the early morning light to find anyone who had been missed in the evacuation. As yet, however, Miranda was far too boisterous to get helicopters aloft.

The dinghy rescuers found themselves in a strange landscape of tree-tops, hillocks crowded with wild and some domestic animals, chimney pots, church towers and occasional roof-tops – with and without waving people – and floating material of all kinds, a picture not unlike 1607 drawings of the Great Flood. The Somerset villages of Thorney and Muchelney among others were almost completely submerged.

With a brief to rescue as many people as was possible before even considering trying to help animals, in the Somerset area alone the dinghy rescuers plucked 25 people of all ages from rooftops and top-floor windows. Four people found swimming bravely towards dry land more than a mile away had been pulled out of the water, all exhausted. And there were, sadly, seven bodies, among them a child of six and an 82-year-old woman – but this was a figure that might rise once the flood had receded enough to allow house-to-house searches. They found they were unable to by-pass some of the animals – a cat crying pitifully in a tree-top, a dog paddling gamely along with no dry land in sight. And finally, they managed to take fodder out to sheep, cows, horses, pigs and wild deer, badgers and foxes on some of the hillocks. Luckily – or rather because of a sterling effort against the clock to move stock to high ground – there were relatively few stranded farm animals. What treetops there were housed scores of bewildered birds of all kinds, including flocks of normally land-dwelling pheasants.

It was much the same picture on the Welsh side of the estuary, with Cardiff itself badly hit and homes along the already-flooded Wye to beyond Redbrook half-submerged. On this side, mercifully, just three people had drowned. So far Miranda had claimed 15 lives overall.

***

Once the surge had wrought its worst on the estuary levels, it moved rapidly up towards an area that was already experiencing its own problems. From Tewkesbury down to Gloucester, the downstream rolling melee of water and debris that had originated in Powys and on Plynlimon trundled along, drawing an ever-widening press of pent-up water behind it. Just as people in Tewkesbury, Gloucestrians had wisely retreated to the higher parts of the city, although almost everybody was up and out in the roaring gale and lashing rain to watch the ongoing spectacle as, quite soon, the Quayside went under, the lock leading into the docks and the Sharpness-Gloucester Canal was overtopped, and College Green and the cathedral itself were close to being invaded. The city's surrounding hams were under several feet of water and the Over Causeway disappeared beneath the surface as did the Gloucester-Cardiff rail line and its iron bridge, also Thomas Telford's preserved but these days unused magnificent stone road bridge. The electricity sub-station on the hams had been wisely taken off-line: although sandbagged to the height of the transformers, it was quickly going under. Like Tewkesbury, Gloucester suddenly became a town without power.

Bad as all this was, once it was obvious that the down-river menace had passed flood-hit Gloucester people started to move cautiously back down to their homes and businesses to assess the damage, only to be met by loudspeaker warnings barked from police vans. The danger, it seemed, was not yet over – a far greater menace would soon be on its way back up the river:

"Stay where you are. This is a serious warning. Within the next two hours a severe tidal surge is expected, and levels are likely to rise further. Anybody who has not found a safe place is risking their life and the lives of others. This is a warning – please stay in a place of safety well away from the river. Keep away from the river! Keep away from the river!"

Chapter 16

John Carter was shaken awake at 3am by the rattle of gravel on his bedroom window. He could have been forgiven for thinking it was heavy rain until he heard shouting.

"Wake up, Johnno, time to get a-rolling."

Tad Morgan again. Suppressing a strong inclination to be grumpy, Carter went downstairs to let the photographer in, directed him to the kitchen to make them both instant coffees and then had a scant wash and pulled on some warm clothes.

"Ready for it?" Tad said when he came back down. "I think it's going to start getting light soon. Or it would if it wasn't for the storm clouds. Get this down you and we'll be off. You want waterproofs too, or you'll be soaked."

"Don't you ever sleep?" was all Carter could comment. It wasn't until they had crossed the Chepstow bridge over the raging Wye and were halfway to Newnham that he felt fully awake. To their right there were occasional glimpses of the estuary basin, now miles wider than normal. "Not a lot of water yet," Carter observed drily. Tad, peering through the rain-dashed windscreen, said nothing.

Soon they were winding up the short corkscrew hill under Newnham churchyard and entering the highest part of the town. They peeled left onto the Green, which was the only way they could go unless they ran into a forbidding line of traffic bollards across the main road.

"I'll park just here on the grass," Tad said, but even as he spoke a policeman in a yellow Hi-Viz jacket stepped into the road and raised a hand to stop him. Tad rolled his window down.

"I'm sorry, Sir..." the policeman started to say, but Tad butted in brightly.

"Hello Roger. Got you up early, have they? Shame."

The policeman smiled suddenly and leaned against the car.

"Tad Morgan. Might have known you'd be here. Look, you won't find anywhere to park that way – the Green's all full of parked cars already and it's the same lower down on the fields by the Freemasons. And for a mile or so out of town, come to that. But I tell you what – we've got the old Victoria Hotel car park to ourselves and the SARA rescue crews. I think I can get you in with us. Just off to your right there, but put your Press card on the dashboard. Say I sent you. Who's that with you, by the way?

"John Carter from the *Clarion*. John, this is DC Roger Bryan, local force."

"Oh aye – another bloody vulture. Can you smell rotting flesh?"

"Very funny," said Tad. "Are you expecting a good show here?"

The policeman frowned. "I've never known anything like it – a bloody disaster, it seems. We have to start shutting the main road. Anybody who comes along will have to park up at the roadside, wherever they are. That'll create a tailback all the way from here back to Chepstow, and in the other direction they expect the road will be impassable all the way to Gloucester. I'd get that car in the Vic's park now before anybody else pinches the spot."

They took his advice without delay. While Tad got his camera gear out of the car, Carter walked back against the wind to the road and the Green. The trees fringing the west-facing side of the natural mound of ground were being lashed furiously by the growing hurricane, and the rain seemed to be heavier now than it had been on the previous evening. To his right on the grass there was a sea of parked cars. He felt Tad tap his elbow.

"C'mon. Let's see if we can find ourselves some loony surfers."

They left the car park and, bent against the weather, set off down Newnham's steep High Street – unlit, for here too the power had gone – and its avenue of limes leading to the unusual clock tower. For the time of day, it was a crowded scene. There was no traffic, and knots of people were gathered in the road – certainly most of the community, plus others who had been stopped by the police from going any further.

From behind them, its sound half blown away by the wind, the church's Victorian carillon chimed a pretty little tune then struck five o'clock.

"An hour to go, perhaps," Tad commented, stopping to take a camera out of his shoulder-slung holdall. He fitted a long lens onto the body, put the camera harness over his shoulder and they continued. Soon they had the lower bend in sight and the mass of Unlawater House and its high-walled raised gardens facing them. Perched near the edge of the wall against mock castellations were two SARA rescue dinghies with their wet-suited volunteer crews beside them. On the rest of the garden there was quite a gallery of onlookers, and every window of the bay-fronted house was also full of spectators.

On the road now the crowds were thicker, and there was a buzz of expectation in the voices around them.

"There! Look!" Tad said suddenly, raising his camera.

A police van and a line of policemen were barricading the bend below the house. Beyond them to their right, across a small visitors' car park, lay the flood defence embankment and the broad bed of the river. Standing silhouetted on the top of the embankment, statue-like, were five bore riders with their long wind-buffeted surfboards held upright beside them, ready for action. Tad stopped and aimed for a long shot that took in the line of police, the car park, and behind them the striking figures and the river. The flashes came quick, one after another.

"Beautiful, that," he said, letting the camera go so that it rested against his stomach. "Exhibition stuff. And your front page, for sure." And he added macabrely: "Before and after, perhaps. First this, then they go on their insane ride, then we get the bodies coming out of the briny. Tragedy in three acts, isn't it?"

Carter shuddered. He'd experienced this apparent cold-heartedness in press photographers before. Perhaps it was the fact that they'd been called out all too often in the middle of the night to photograph bodies being cut out of car wrecks. And work had been even more traumatic, perhaps, for Tad – as a young photographer he had been one of the first pressmen to reach Aberfan.

Carter pushed his way through the crowd towards the police line to see if he could wheedle his way into getting a word with the surfers, Tad just behind him.

"Careful, Johnno, I don't know this lot," the Welshman hissed. "Drafted in from Gloucester or Stroud I bet – maybe even Cheltenham, somewhere wild and uncivilised like that. Be polite."

The cops were standing stiffly in a row, hands clasped behind their backs and trying not to mind the wind and wet. They'd obviously been told to look stern but not threatening. Behind them was a black-moustached Super, a bit overweight, pacing up and down the line. Carter took out his press card and held it so that the chief could see it.

"Press, Superintendent – can we come through? We want to talk with the bore-riders please."

Untrustingly the Super reached between two of his men to take the card. He examined it closely, as if he'd never seen a press card before, but Carter wasn't fooled by this obvious piece of power-play.

"What paper are you from, son?"
Be polite...
"The Clarion, Sir – it's our area."

The man passed the card back slowly. Was he going to be difficult?

"What good would it be to talk to them? I don't want them there, but they're too stubborn to move."

"It's public interest, Sir. You'll find the card says the police can cooperate with us."

The small print on the back only said the holder was recognised by the police as a bona-fide newsman – nothing about cooperation. But the Super nodded.

"Very well. Just five minutes with them, that's all, then you come back off that bank and move well up the town out of the way. I don't want to be held responsible for your safety, is that clear?"

"Got that, Sir."

Carter turned and gave Tad a covert wink and they both slipped through the line, but before they could go any further the Super put a hand on Carter's arm. His tone became friendlier.

"See if you can stop those bloody fools going through with this, eh? They're going to be killed for sure if what I've heard about this surge-thing is true. I've tried hard enough but they won't see reason. Can you have a go?"

"I will, Sir, but I don't hold out much hope."

"Good lad," said the Super, as if he was talking to one of his own men. But as Tad and Carter squelched their way across the gravelled car park to the embankment, he shouted after them.

"Five minutes!"

The storm struck them all the harder as they climbed to the top of the bank and approached the riders. Alan Jenkins, in the middle of them, smiled when he saw who it was.

"John Carter, heh? Knew you'd come. Did they give you a hard time too down there? Right lot of killjoys."

Carter shrugged. "They think they're trying to save your worthless lives," he said. "Not such a bad motive, really, is it?"

Jenkins steadied his board against a punch of wind. "But you're not going to try as well now, are you?"

"I'll admit there's a certain futility in that. But perhaps you'd like to tell me how you're going to handle something as big as this – something people have never seen, let alone thought about."

"You want to know our plan?"

"Okay."

"Well, basically, as soon as this thing arrives and we can judge the size of it, we hitch a ride keeping quite wide of the middle on this side, towards the Broadoak bank, but then we cut the other way to get under the Arlingham bank. We can then go on up to Minsterworth, with luck, and maybe further. But Arlingham is our escape plan. If we get into any trouble we can beach and wait for smooth water to paddle back home. Simple."

"You don't know what you're in for," said Carter. "You've heard about the muck coming downriver – looks like you're going to meet that pretty soon."

Jenkins nodded. "Look out there," he said, sweeping his hand round the view across the estuary. "There's all sorts of stuff already here from the last tide. I can see beer kegs, pub tables, tree trunks, fish, dead animals, all in this one little bit alone. But we've ridden in flood conditions before, and you'll notice that all the debris is in the narrow channel where the river runs between sandbanks at low tide. It continues along that line when the water comes up, so if you keep well clear of it you shouldn't hit trouble. Yes, we have to go across it at some point, but..."

He shrugged, not finishing.

One of the other surfers piped up, humorously.

"Would you care to join us?"

"Ha ha," Carter laughed grimly. There was nothing funny about the situation. He looked from one face to the other.

"I suppose I'm wasting my time trying. I reckon the only soundbite I can get out of this is that you all went into the water not really knowing what you would face, but that you were as prepared as you could be for the worst. Would it be fair to say that? And that you'd been told your lives were in danger but decided to ignore it?"

Some shrugged, and he could see most of them agreed with his summary even if he was putting words into their mouths. Jenkins said: "If you're looking for a quote, say that we are taking Miranda on in the spirit of Mad Jack Churchill. That's what we've posted on our Longwave website – take a look."

Carter looked him in the eye. "Okay, I'll use that. And I – we – should wish you luck. How long before the bore arrives now?"

Jenkins turned into the wind, lifted his face, his long locks fluttering pennant-like behind him.

"I'd say she's already on her way. I can feel her coming, can't you? Early – what you'd expect with a big following wind. You can feel the tide pushing the airflow, you know. All that water flooding in displaces the air in the valley and funnels it this way. It's building up now, so I'd say we've about half an hour to get into position. In fact, we ought to move now." Then he raised his voice for his fellow boarders: "Are we all ready?"

"Not a lot of light," Tad grumbled. He braced himself with one leg down the bank and took several side-shots as the surfers made their way down its slope to the riverbed and set out, wading warily at first, towards the middle. When they reached lagoons of puddled water, they laid their boards flat, stretched out on them and began to paddle with their hands, looking for all the world like a group of little hatchling turtles heading for the ocean.

The thought struck Carter that this might be the last anyone ever saw of them…

The police started barking orders through a megaphone for onlookers to back further up the town. The Super caught his eye and gave an exaggerated sweeping arm gesture that was quite clear: get off the bank!

As he and the photographer made their way down Carter too felt the change in the air. It was colder now, stronger but steadier. It smelled of the sea.

On the 'safe' side of the flood bank the pressmen pushed back into the crowd, but it was clear they would get very little sight of the river if they were in the thick of it so Carter suggested to Tad that they try to get to the Unlawater House lawn. With that objective in mind they edged towards the back of the large building with the hope of getting round the blind side first. It was a bit of a struggle, but they finally managed it with a bit of help from a local policeman who recognised Tad and let him through the mainly hostile police barrier. At the request of the flat owners in the former mansion, a 'no entry' area had been extended virtually all around the house. There was, however, little that could be done to shift the people already there.

"Local knowledge, see," grinned the photographer as they crossed the garden. "If it was my house, I'd have been charging tickets. I reckon we'll be best off by the lifeboats at the riverside edge of the garden. What do you think? The crews have got a bit of a clearing roped off over there – and probably the best view."

The two came in for some banter when they reached the lifeboat crews – three men to each boat. Again, Tad knew most of them quite well, as did Carter, though less so. They were used to having pressmen see them off and back in again after a rescue. They'd sometimes give their boats a bit more gun on the 'in' run as they neared the land, purely for the benefit of cameramen – a practice that would probably be frowned upon by the chiefs of the RNLI, but as an independent volunteer charity SARA was a little more liberal about that sort of thing. Today they were quite happy to have the press team in the little enclave protected by the police.

"Lovely day for it!" Tad quipped as a fierce wet squall off the river drummed on the rubber dinghies.

The front of the elevated lawn was, as Tad had suggested, an ideal grandstand for looking out across the estuary. This morning, in the beating rain, they could now just see the tiny figures of the bore-riders, up to their waists in the water, boards beside them. To their left, had it been a clear day, they could have seen the spire of Westbury church, miles away and rising above the abrupt right hand bend in the still-broad river by the tiny hamlet of Broadoak, which lay between them. To the right lay Newnham on its high knoll topped by St Peter's with its quarter-chiming clock, and across the water was the low, flat shore of the Arlingham Peninsula, now just visible. In Roman times there had been a low-tide ford across here, and even in more recent times a rowing-boat ferry.

SARA lifeboat chief Bert Windsor was taking a lengthy mobile phone call and looking worried.

"That was the next unit a bit down the coast," he said when he'd finished. "I don't think anyone up here is going to be safe, from what I've heard. Looks like we're going to have to clear even this area – except for us, of course."

As he walked to the edge of the wall Carter said quickly to Tad: "I wonder if the 'we' includes us?" Tad shrugged.

"Superintendent!" Windsor bawled down into the gale.

The policeman moved nearer.

"Superintendent, I've just spoken to some of our crews off Chepstow and over at Weston and it's already far worse than anyone had imagined. You'll have to get people further back up into town and even clear most of them off this garden. It's going to be huge and it's going to come in fast."

Instinctively the policeman below them looked over his shoulder at the tiny figures of the bore riders in the middle of the estuary, then back at the lifeboat chief. "What about..." he started to say, but he was cut short by the man's shrug of resignation.

"We'll never reach them in time. We'd all be killed."

"Okay. I'll start moving people now. I'll send someone up to you to help there."

"Good," said the lifeboatman. "And I should get your vehicles off the car park and up that road too if you want to see them tomorrow."

As if to emphasise the point, there was a brilliant flash of blue and purple lightning from downriver, followed by a deep, menacing rumble of thunder.

Surfer Alan Jenkins had started his working life as a salmon fisherman, just like his dad. When he was growing up they had a rank of putchers – conical willow basket fish traps – jutting out into the river, and sometimes he and his father would wade out in shallow water on low tides with big triangular long-handled 'lave' nets, scooping running salmon that were trying to pass them and head on upriver. And sometimes, especially when he was younger, he was a 'runner', scooting on foot for miles along the low-tide sandbanks keeping his sharp eyes wide open to spot stranded fish before the gulls and ravens got to them.

He loved the hollow-sounding noise his running footsteps made on the packed wet sand, but on one eerie occasion – when he was ten or thereabouts – he'd found himself caught in a sudden mist mid-river, a miasma that was full of ghosts and voices and unknown horrors. It chilled him to his core, and he knew he had to run and run blindly until he could escape. He never knew how far he went, but eventually he collapsed, exhausted, and started to lose consciousness. When he came-to he was lying on a sandbank in warm sunshine accompanied by a lone, puzzled-looking seagull. All around there were familiar landmarks and he walked thankfully home along the riverbed.

He had stuck with the fishing while his father was alive, which was to his sixteenth birthday. Even back then the big runs of migratory salmon had started to dwindle, especially the multi-return big fish that would maintain good stocks of the species. Gone too, it appeared, were the huge armour-plated sturgeon they sometimes encountered. Once, he and Dad found a big one, maybe 100lb, with its head stuck in a putcher. The Queen's fish, his dad had said, we're supposed to take them to Her Majesty.

"What shall we do now?" his son asked when they'd beached the monster.

"Put 'un back," said his Dad. "Let somebody else worry about that."

The old man went out quickly with a lung embolism, just 48. Somehow fishing didn't have either the appeal or indeed much of a future after that. But by then he'd also caught the bore-riding bug, and he realised he could never be far from the river he loved and knew so much about. Often when he was out in the middle of the river, waiting to catch a 'ride on the tide', he would think of those early fishing days with fondness. He still had the eyes to scan the shallow water for the weaving fin of a salmon zig-zagging upstream, and such sights always brought to mind an image of his Dad, out there with his lave net, waiting to make the riverman's traditional high-stepping run to snare a silver darling.

Even today, waiting for this big bore, Alan was still at that level of watchful awareness.

He looked round at his companions. Two were old friends with long experience like him, and two were younger, but he'd seen enough of them in action to know that they could handle a rough ride. And a rough ride it very likely would be – certainly nothing like the bores any of them had been used to, either here or on raging foreign rivers.

He felt the water swell suddenly, starting to inch up his legs, and the wind stiffened further. Screwing up his eyes he tried, like the others, to see through the murk what sort of a demon was coming at them from downstream. A thrumming sensation came through the soles of his feet, faint at first but growing. It was on its way – and now he knew just where it was, gathering all its strength in the huge basin just below the church, forming a violently spinning maelstrom of angry sand-laden brown water and giving out a roar that sounded as if the very earth was being ripped apart.

It was just around the corner, just up there...

Time to get ready...

The moment of truth...

At first the bore looked just like a wall barging its way up the river – a big, solid black wall. Bores before had looked like that, but it was only when it was about 300 yards away and licking the walls of riverside village houses as it advanced that he realised the true size of this one, how steep it was, and how it was rippling over the tide defence bank of the Arlingham side, spreading out over the flat land. It was huge, as was the mountain of water towering behind it. He was looking at an intimidating eighteen, twenty, even more feet.

Too late to cut and run, even if he'd wanted to. Too late too to wonder exactly how to tackle such an immense problem. All he could do was rely on his wits and let instinct cut in.

The others were all on their boards now, paddling for all their worth to get up enough speed for the water to bear them aloft on its sloping forward edge and start to carry them along. Alan threw his board down and fell on it, started to paddle as if his very life depended upon it, which in all probability it did.

Chapter 17

At the Portishead nerve centre of Operation Sandbag there had been a sudden break from the patient, methodical mapping of the developing situation as reports started to come in that acres of low-lying land encircling the police HQ were flooding rapidly. Many moved to the windows hoping for a glimpse of the incursion. Disappointingly, all they could see was a dark landscape of storm-lashed silhouetted trees, but when they went back to their tasks many had a strange sensation that they were actually now on an island, cut off from the rest of the world...

Then the alarmed phone calls started to come in thick and fast, from the mouth of the Bristol Avon that wound its way under a high M5 bridge just to the north of Portishead, and on the Welsh side of the Severn from Cardiff's Ely River and the Taff, from the Usk through Newport, and from the Wye Valley – all rivers that were already overburdened after days of unbroken heavy rain.

At Bristol city itself, the surge took many by surprise as it raced up the Avon Gorge under Brunel's historic Clifton suspension bridge. Luckily the Portway main road beside the river had been closed to traffic, just in time for it was quickly under several feet of rushing water which moved on to Cumberland Basin and the Floating Harbour and the broad anchorage of the city's centre. From here one branch washed over harbour walls to the footings of offices and homes, in some instances emptying into their lower floors, and another took the rushing floodwater along the old Feeder Canal almost up to Temple Meads railway station. After this the flows merged into one and the upstream torrent simply overwhelmed the downstream flow and showed contempt for weirs at Hanham and Keynsham where there was, in any case, very little 'fall' left. It moved on to Saltford and it rushed over already-waterlogged meadows towards Bath, beyond which the river valley walls narrowed and steepened.

Large areas of Cardiff between the Taff and the Ely suffered a similar fate, with water then racing on up the river valleys to inundate fields and properties. In Newport it was touch and go whether it would do widespread damage to the town, but upstream water swelled over riverside acres almost to Usk town. The surge on the Wye rubbed at the solid stone bulwarks of Chepstow's Norman castle, then swept across the Lancaut Peninsula rather than taking its usual route around the promontory. Then it pushed on up against an already widespread flood to Redbrook, normally the upper tidal reach, and beyond.

Operation Sandbag staff were reminded from time to time that it wasn't just the floodwater they had to contend with. Miranda's ferocious wind squalls were bringing down trees, ripping off roofs and bowling over vehicles and people. Power outages were starting to become widespread. In the light of this, the decision was taken to start up the HQ emergency generator and switch to this sure supply.

Caroline Cleaver, like Mike Winter, wore a telephone headset that kept her in constant communication with Mervyn Connor at the Met HQ in Exeter, and her job was passing on storm information to the group gathered around the situation map. Mike's 'new' but temporary job was to send reports of the storm's effects back to Connor and other staff down in Devon.

Caroline was rather glad she hadn't brought her knitting along. The situation was turning out to be a little too busy for that.

"Mervyn Connor says we should be very near the thick of it now. Things are starting to clear up in Exeter, weather-wise at least," she reported to Christine Lees, who was still on her feet and seemingly indefatigable. "We should be through the worst in about an hour and a half, two hours, but he says we shouldn't expect appreciable amounts of the water to simply disappear any time soon. It might even be after the next high that any run-off is noticed. There's an unprecedented amount of backed-up water out there pressing against us, and it can only dissipate gradually westwards, into the Atlantic. Does that make sense?"

The policewoman nodded and turned to Michael Saunders of the Environment Agency – one of the operation team who really did look weary – and said: "Shall I arrange some accommodation for us all? The lead players anyway. I think we're going to have to break the operation into shifts."

Saunders agreed. Gladly, Caroline thought. The policewoman called a mini huddle to discuss how the break-up might be done. She also reported more deaths – an old man who had been bedridden in the upper rooms of his Somerset home and one of three children, all aged about ten, who had been discovered drifting inexplicably across a flooded field near Caldicot holding onto a garish pink and yellow toy sea monster.

Connor was glad when the worst weather that had reached Somerset appeared to have blown through. However, the southern branch of the surge's romp eastwards along the South Devon shore and the English Channel was still leaving a trail of mayhem.

At Hallsands, where in 1917 the whole village had been swept away in a January storm, there was relief the rebuilt community was higher-up and more secure, but at Dawlish, where the shoreline railway plunged picturesquely in and out of tunnels through red sandstone cliffs, a whole section of the rebuilt track (washed away once before in a 2014 storm) was again lost to the sea – cutting the mainline rail link westwards.

All in all, most places, including Exeter itself, had prepared well despite having little time to do so. There were already casualties in this region of course – two dead and several injured from falling trees in Cornwall, and in Dorset a man had undoubtedly drowned (body so far not recovered) after being plucked by a wave from Chesil beach.

There was also widespread boat damage – thousands and thousands of pounds-worth – as the surge carried on to the Isle of Wight and the Solent, to Portsmouth, Brighton, Eastbourne, Dover, into the Thames estuary and up to a frightening level on the raised barrage walls. Seaside properties and businesses took a battering too, but that things weren't far worse was a tribute to the work put in by Michael Saunders and his staff at the Environment Agency. They had seen that sea defences were as robust as they possibly could be given that money for this was always tight.

Connor's main concern, however, was still the main branch of Miranda's continued progress north east. She had vented her fury on the vulnerable Somerset coast and South Wales and at this very moment she was probably centred almost exactly above Operation Sandbag HQ up in Portishead. And the surge was about to clash with another considerable force when it raced, as predicted, up the narrowing Severn estuary. The upshot of this event had been highly unpredictable all along.

***

From their raised vantage point on the Unlawater House lawn, John Carter and Tad Morgan were overawed (as was everybody else) by the sheer size of the surge roaring towards them up the river. In seconds they were up to their knees in water, and the SARA lifeboats were afloat with their crews clambering aboard. Behind them, up Newnham's main street, police and onlookers alike were scrabbling to get away from the water and up to higher ground. To the north of them, towards Broadoak, and east, where the Arlingham peninsula once lay, there was an unbroken sweep of rapidly spreading water. Tad was still clicking away – shots of the river and the panic-ridden town street – but it was becoming clear they were personally in trouble. As locals, they knew the water would rise further. Carter took his photographer's arm and started to steer him towards the town and higher ground, but there was a sudden shout behind them.

"Over here!"

The water was up over the footings of the big house and the doorstep was almost disappearing, but the door was half-open, and somebody was beckoning from inside. Gratefully they sploshed towards the entrance and stepped in. Their saviour was on the stairs ahead of them, still beckoning as they spluttered their thanks. They followed him up to a hallway leading into a first floor sitting room with a large window overlooking the flood.

"I'd take those wet things off," said the elderly gentleman in a fawn cardigan and red felt carpet-slippers. "Here." He passed them some towels, while Carter introduced himself and Tad.

"Press men eh? Thought you were. Richard Soames. I was a reporter once, believe it or not, but now it's rather nice to be retired and writing true romances – just to keep my hand in of course. See, there is life at the end of the tunnel! Come over to the window. This is all too good to miss. A tragedy, but I doubt if I'll ever see anything like it again in my lifetime. Nor will you, I hope."

They looked out. The SARA boats had their engines gunned and were idling nose against the flow to hold position roughly where the car park lay under several feet of water.

"Did you see the surfers?" Carter asked. "Did you see what happened to them? Did they make it?"

Their host was shaking his head.

"I saw them get on their boards. But the water came up so high and so quickly it was impossible to see them after that. I don't give them much of a chance in this, do you? Mad as a sack of frogs."

Carter and Morgan had seen no more of the bore riders than their new friend they told him. Tad took more shots through the window, then turned to speak to the other two.

"You'd better come over and look. It's getting a bit Biblical out there."

***

After the River Severn's eastern arm had submerged low-lying areas of Gloucester before reuniting with the main stream, the great downward swell of water and its flowing bridal train of debris had kept on widening and spreading out over the meadows to either side. It left a trail of damage as it progressed, ripping out bankside trees and bushes before swamping Minsterworth's slaughterhouse and pub. The floods kept swelling over the estuary's first wide sands at Rodley. Here, the A48 road left the riverside and climbed steeply to Chaxhill, and with low-lying land to the west – an area often flooded in winter but normally dry through summer – as well as eastwards along the river meadows, a large island started to form from Minsterworth's fringe to Westbury Garden Cliff further down the Severn. Below this island a truly unexpected and alarming 'water feature' had started to form.

Ahead of the bore, the growing tide was starting to back up water against the main flow and soon two juggernauts, one heading upstream and one downstream, were on a collision course…

An Environment Agency regional officer might have been the first to entertain the puzzle of what might happen if an irresistible force met an immovable object. Now, watchers on the Chaxhill 'island' vantage point had one answer playing out before their very eyes. The two huge currents first tried to skirt one another, each finding what seemed a path of least resistance. For moments it seemed as if this would work for them, with driven water spilling away to either side, but then to the amazement of horrified onlookers they bit into one another, as if trying to chase each others' tails, and formed a huge, rapidly-growing cartwheeling whirlpool accompanied by a chilling deep-throated roar.

Connor would say later that the area of extreme low atmospheric pressure above the new monster had perhaps helped it to gain this momentum. Whatever, the fury set off downriver scooping everything off the banks that dared to stand in its way. Down and down it whirled, getting bigger by the minute, down to where a group of boarders had just caught the upstream surf break of their lives.

***

Alan Jenkins was crouched low when he felt the sudden shove of water and he shifted his centre of balance forward on his board so that he was riding – and riding fast – down the face of the bore wave. This was the point in most bore rides that he would usually think of standing – but this time he had not taken on an ordinary bore. It was a monster.

A quick glance showed there were two others riding with him, Knapp and Vincent he thought, but what had happened to the other two was anybody's guess. Both the successful riders were still not standing up, but holding on tight, probably just as terrified as he was.

The deep growl behind was now almost deafening. To either side he could see nothing of the riverbanks, just rushing water, apparently endless in every direction, supporting the three of them. "*Go with the flow*," a voice inside him urged, "It has to be heading somewhere if you stay with it." But never had he felt his life – and the lives of the other riders – to be in so much danger. Too late for regrets. "*Go with the flow*," the voice urged again, and he found himself mouthing the words over and over, a mantra.

But then something very strange happened: the wave collapsed, the huge bank of water behind him slowed and stopped as if it was having second thoughts about its headlong career. He toppled in.

Only then did he see the edge of the giant whirlpool bearing down on him from upstream, its foaming edge spitting spray and its deep growl growing louder and louder. He was now trapped in a deep trough between immense bodies of moving water. There was no time to ponder what might happen, just time to throw himself across his board and hang on for dear life as he was plunged into a confusing melee. Bobbing up like a cork briefly, he managed to snatch a look around to see what was happening. Any hope of salvation faded immediately. He was circling in a truly-enormous enlarged vortex formed by the two forces, each of them now being fed by even more water – the surge tide and the massive Severn flood. And his board was speeding up. He realised with horror he was being drawn towards the deep, rubbish-filled centre while, perversely, the whirlpool had now started moving upstream and was accelerating.

He had seen whirlpools before in the Severn. One of these – quite a large and frightening one – would regularly form in the basin below Newnham's St Peter's Church where it could be watched from the safety of the clifftop iron rail fence of the graveyard on the knoll. It would grow into a helter-skelter fury with a big tide and would last for several minutes before slowly subsiding. Watching, you would be very glad you were not caught up in it, swimming for your life. But in case you were, Alan Jenkins reminded himself, his late father the salmon-fisher had given him a sage piece of old riverman's advice: "*Let it take you down. Don't try to fight it, because you can't, and you'll just die. Let it swallow you and take breaths when you can. It has to spit you out somewhere and you can be sure it will.*"

But it was hard not to give in to dread, feel done-for, defeated, without hope. Were any of the others in there with him? If they were, he couldn't make them out. All manner of things kept appearing and disappearing in the muddy, rumbling depths as he sank lower and lower. In a matter of minutes, he was at the centre, deep and dark under the overcast skies. The board slid from under him, but he could feel it was still attached to his ankle-cord. He stuck his arms out in a vain attempt to keep afloat but he was soon up to his neck, going under ... then there was a rush of gritty, sand-filled water over his head and sudden compression in his ears that told him he was still going on down. He held his breath for as long as he could. Then he blacked out.

Minutes after the bore riders had set out on their reckless journey the two SARA lifeboats were able to batter their way out into the massively swollen – and still rising – river, using full power to keep their heads into the tide but allowing themselves to drift back slowly with the current to the two flailing boarders who had failed to catch the wave. They got both of them into one boat, the other standing by as backup, then made all haste back to the road under Unlawater House, dropping the two exhausted men safely up Newnham's High Street, where sightseers crowded at the water's edge had to back up further to make room for them. SARA's volunteer first responder checked the two casualties over. Both were exhausted and cold but had no visible injuries.

Still grumbling about the poor light, Tad Morgan took some shots of the rescue from the pressmen's vantage point in the flats.

"I'll put the kettle on. Tea, anyone?" said their host when the drama was over.

"Wait!" said Tad. "Something's happening. Oh, my dear Lord, will you look at that?"

Sensing the awe in his voice Richard Soames and John Carter went back to the window to look upstream at the approaching, swirling water.

"Have you ever, ever seen anything like that?" Tad asked, suddenly remembering to take more shots. Soon, he thought, it would be right under their noses. He might be the only press photographer to capture this phenomenon. He might be able to make a book, or even get an exhibition about this when it was all over!

But the circling monster didn't get any closer. It stopped. And then, slowly at first but inexorably, it started to move away, upriver, still spinning, driven by the huge amount of water that kept on rising behind it.

"That's going to be a real nuisance," said Carter. "Gloucester and Tewkesbury are already expected to be flooded by now. If this pushes on all the way up there it can only add to their problems. A bloody catastrophe."

He hoped Phyllis was still well away from it all near Mitcheldean. If she could get up Plump Hill, she would find the vale below looking very different from a few days ago – a vast lake stretching almost as far as the Cotswold scarp.

***

The Operation Sandbag team at Portishead was now minus Michael Saunders, Mike Winter, one of the three Army representatives and three policemen, who had all been sent off to hastily arranged camp beds in a rest-room for a couple of hours' sleep. Chief Constable Christine Lees remained in charge but would be relieved by Saunders when the rested team came back. Reports from around the country told her the other operation centres were coping well, and she was relieved she didn't have the responsibility for all those areas too. Right now there was something of a hiatus as they swung from trying to protect people to getting them out of any trouble they found themselves in. This, the rescue phase, could last for hours and perhaps even days as squads searched for any problems. To assist them, search and rescue helicopters were already up from Bristol Lulsgate airport, scouring the flooded landscape as Miranda headed on across the country towards East Anglia, mercifully weakening as she progressed.

On the operations table the coastline of the British Isles had changed dramatically, if only temporarily, the most staggering incursions being into large swathes of Somerset, Gloucestershire and South Wales. The upper Gloucestershire section was still very much active as the tide continued on its path up the Severn. Most of the rest of Britain's coast looked as if it had been nibbled off here and there by some leviathan, while parts of the East Coast were still bracing themselves for the worst.

"How much water do you think all that is, as a matter of interest? Is there any way of measuring it?" the Chief Constable asked meteorologist Caroline Cleaver, sweeping her hand over the flood area.

Cleaver shook her head. "It's nearly impossible to tell. You could try breaking it up into sydharbs, I suppose, but I still don't think you'd come very close."

"Sydharbs? What are they?"

"Sydharbs are hypothetical measurements much frowned upon in serious discourse by people in the water business. Don't laugh, but a sydharb is the amount of water in Sydney Harbour at high tide. Or roughly 562,000 megalitres.

There was a rare laugh from Christine Lees.

"So, if I ask you how many sydharbs we're looking at here, your answer would probably be 'lots'. Am I right?"

Cleaver smiled. By degrees, the at-first stern guardian of the law was turning out to be human, even likeable.

"Pretty much," she said, "give or take a couple of litres here and there."

***

In Exeter Mervyn Connor had also set himself the mental task of trying to measure the vast amount of water that had made its way over formerly dry land, and the term 'sydharb' had crossed his mind briefly too. He was thinking about this because he had been asked (with Michael Saunders) to present the Prime Minister with salient facts so that she could give an official government response to the disaster. Part of that request was to provide an assessment of what might be done to alleviate any future flooding and storm damage on such a scale. This was much more Saunders' area of expertise than his own, for it was the Environment Agency's responsibility to maintain flood defences and, if necessary, strengthen them. Reading between the lines of the e-mailed request, he detected first an appeal to him and Saunders to predict if such a storm as Miranda was ever likely to strike again (and if so, when), and secondly to provide a good reason for everyone being caught napping when the catastrophe blew in. '*Can the warnings come any earlier?*' it seemed to be asking.

On that last point he muttered to himself, "I wish," but he had a lot of relevant thoughts about climate change which he was sure would make uncomfortable reading for the country's lords and masters up in Westminster. That matter would have to wait until he had a good sit-down session with Saunders, who would have to go cap-in-hand to the Treasury in order to get an extra metre put on a flood bank here, or deeper dredged channels there. In all probability his suggestions would then be rejected by the bean-counters of Whitehall as being too expensive to contemplate.

The question of 'how much water' was a tricky one, but possibly not insoluble. Measure the flooded ground area by the depth of water, taking contours into account, and you could come up with an answer, give or take a few thousand sydharbs. If you fed a computer with the right information you might get a more accurate figure – but in any case, at this point the progress of the flooding was far from over.

However, he made a mental note to himself to try to get his maths experts to invent a computer programme that would marry contour maps with water depths to get quick answers on quantities.

That would have to wait until this was all over. Right now, he really needed to talk to Saunders, but first he needed a vital update on Miranda's current status.

A man called Brian Robinson had taken Mike Winter's place at Exeter. He was older, but just as capable. On his desk screen, a much-diminished spider's web of lines was just moving across the bulge of East Anglia's coast. Fronts trailed down to the Home Counties where they were undoubtedly delivering heavy rain, while to the west there were few features for some distance other than a growing ridge of high pressure. Things would be calming down when that arrived. Connor pointed at the depression moving towards the North Sea.

"That's Miranda?"

Robinson nodded. "She's a bit more manageable now. Spent force, maybe."

"I'll say," Connor agreed. "Do you mind running a sequence as far back as we can go? I want to see if there are any early signs of her that we missed."

Robinson got his computer to reverse the satellite images of now-dwindling Miranda's track, back to where she romped destructively through the Midlands, back further to where she had savaged the west coast and unleashed a huge tidal surge, back again to the west of Ireland where she first gathered her forces under a full moon, and back further still towards America where there was an apparently empty sea, weather-wise, save for the tiniest squiggle, so insignificant it was not surprising it had been overlooked.

"Stop," said Connor, "I think that's it. So small we haven't bothered to give it a pressure reading. Do you know what I think it is?

"Sir?"

"Remnants of a hurricane that's blown through the Caribbean and all the way up the coast of America, where she became a rain depression before becoming spent, or it was assumed so – only in this case she's found the warm, wet waters of the gulf stream, which is just what any respectable hurricane needs. She's recharging here, feeding..." He knocked a knuckle on the screen squiggle, "...without a doubt." He rubbed his temples, frowning.

"Are you all right sir?"

He snapped out of dark thoughts. "Yes, thanks Mr Robinson. Just got more explaining to do than I'd imagined. And I'm a bit tired. Quite a lot tired, in fact.

"Carry on watching the current situation, eh, and let me know if Miranda does anything unexpected ... though I think she's done her worst."

"Will do, Mr Connor."

The chief lingered for a moment, and then said: "Did anyone ever tell you that meteorology isn't an exact science?"

"I have heard that."

"Let's hope everyone else has heard it too."

Connor went to his own desk and called Portishead to arrange the meeting with Saunders he'd been thinking about, only to find from the operation's liaison officer that he was resting and unavailable 'except in the most extreme circumstances'.

"Mr Winter, then, or Mrs Cleaver?"

"I'll see."

There was a pause, then he was clicked through to Caroline. He asked her for an update on the progress of the surge.

"Still very much active, sir. And doing something strange, according to reports. It's formed what looks like a massive whirlpool, heading upriver against a considerable down-flow. Our policeman on the spot at Newnham says it's quite frightening to look at."

Connor tried to picture the situation while opening a map on his own screen.

"That can happen when you get two strong streams running in opposite directions – they're pulled into a vortex, with the strongest force of course eventually dominant. What's the position of the main body of water now? I'm looking at the area myself on-screen."

It was just moving upstream over Rodley sands, she reported, and about to funnel into the narrower section of the riverbed. Behind it, the whole of the Arlingham peninsula appeared to have been submerged, with only trees, a couple of rooftops and a church spire visible from the Newnham side of the river, where there was higher ground.

"I hope everyone knows what's coming their way," he said. "How are we doing on the casualty front so far?"

"I'm sorry to say our Portishead area body count is up to fifteen already. Plus, we've got three surfers missing at Newnham – hard to say if they've survived.

"*Surfers*? What the hell are they doing out in this? They didn't really try to ride the bore, did they?"

"I'm afraid so. Five of them. They've got two out, half-drowned, and the others have disappeared. Everybody tried to stop them going in, apparently. Have you got more fatalities too?"

Added to his list was a woman in Cornwall who had been killed when her car hit a fallen tree – probably driving too fast for the conditions, he commented, adding "There are dramas at sea, too, as you might expect. Unresolved so far. Boats that rode out the bad weather are starting to come in now the wind is dropping. If we can keep the body count to this sort of level it will be a bloody miracle."

He asked Caroline to get Saunders to call him urgently when he was back from his break then rang off.

***

Alan Jenkins blinked his eyes open and lifted his head. His lower half was in water, how deep he couldn't tell, and he was still clutching his surfboard. Somehow, he'd hung on. But he hurt all over.

Around him was a sea of floating debris – plastic containers of all kinds, metal beer casks, tree stumps and branches, picnic tables, a capsized punt and a dead cow, horribly bloated with its legs sticking in the air. Then he saw a surfboard in the middle of it all with a human body face-down beside it, limp, immobile, obviously dead. From the clothing he knew it was without doubt Pete Knapp, one of his closest surfing friends. The sight made him shudder. Of Cec Vincent there was no sign. Had he met a similar fate?

He put a hand up to rub a throbbing area over his left eyebrow and found he was bleeding badly from a gash there;

some of the blood was running down the side of his nose, dripping on his board and splashing into the water to spread and dissolve.

He carefully checked himself all over for any more injuries – just grazes, a few cuts, nothing serious. However, his legs and arms felt leaden. They had no strength left in them. He looked around, beyond the mess he was centred in, to see if he could locate where he was.

Some way off – half a mile maybe? – there was what looked like a low shoreline, and beyond it some houses, and the spire of a church. Westbury, perhaps? Arlingham? He screwed his eyes up to concentrate on the distant bank where he thought he saw a movement.

Was there somebody waving there? There was also what could be the end of a road, and on it a vehicle – a vehicle with a blue flashing light. An ambulance?

Wearily he raised himself as high as he could and lifted an exhausted arm to wave.

Then he collapsed back on his board, uncertain if he'd been seen, closed his eyes and muttered some childhood prayers to Matthew, Mark, Luke and John and all the saints that ever were to keep him alive, help him endure.

What seemed an eternity later he heard the methodical dip, dip, dip of oars and felt the water rippling around him. Hands took his arms and legs, unclipped his board tether and hauled him, half unconscious, into a dinghy and laid him on the bottom. There were more oar dips, then Peter's body appeared, cold and limp, beside him.

"Sorry to have to take you both together," a voice said, "no time for a return trip. Try to lie still. We'll soon have you safe."

And then the tone of voice changed suddenly to one of anger, as if the speaker could no longer be constrained: "What the fuck do you think you were doing out there in this, you silly bastard? Making everyone risk their lives for you. What the fuck?"

But then another more cautious voice cut in.

"Steady, Roger. He's an injured man, remember. And he's just lost his mate here. Let him be."

Chapter 18

As Connor predicted, the surge up the Severn met the narrowing of the banks with an audible slam that shook the ground, great undulating waves of water roaring between already-overtopped flood banks, charging like an express train and spreading outwards from its main flow over a broad front. It easily doubled the three feet of water already covering the A48 road at Elmore Back and charged on to Maisemore and Hempsted, pushing even more water onto the surrounding land as it went. When it reached the outskirts of Gloucester the Blackfriars branch poured into the docks, lifting narrowboats and other pleasure craft, canal dredgers and two tall ships waiting to go in the dry dock perilously close to the top of the dock walls. Extra water drove up the Gloucester-Sharpness Canal. In a pincer movement the main flow that usually bypassed the town to the west poured across the flooded hams and surrounded the electricity sub-station, reuniting the water masses. In no time at all onlookers in the town all saw the water from the Quay rising further up Westgate towards the Cathedral precinct.

At the causeway at Over the supercharged flow first rocked the Gloucester-Cardiff railway bridge then quite suddenly ripped most of the iron structure away, leaving only twisted rails. The old Telford stone bridge trembled, but held, as did the newer bypass road bridge, but the water's movement was just as fast and strong as it drove past Maisemore and on up to Tewkesbury – a town already flooded to the ancient Abbey footings and by and large totally evacuated except for the Bishop, with other cassocked churchmen and the town mayor, watching proceedings from the tower.

It quickly overtopped Tewkesbury's weir – in normal times the limit of tidal water – as if there had been no obstruction whatsoever, and overflowed into the backwater and marina at the mouth of the Warwickshire Avon, floating more pleasure boats off their mooring poles and sending riverside caravans sailing into hedges. Once again, the water treatment plant at Mythe that supplied a huge area including Cheltenham was inundated and inoperable as the surge passed through evacuated Upton before finally losing some of its impetus. It was, however, still a *force majeure* in preventing the outflow for thousands of acres of flooded land for many miles upstream.

***

It was impossible for the team at Portishead to put its finger precisely on the time when the incursions stopped, for there were still many separate incidents of banks giving way here and there and backed-up tributaries suddenly disgorging huge amounts of water. By about four o'clock in the afternoon, however, it was generally assumed that the worst was over – except that there were now thousands and thousands of acres covered in floodwater that wasn't going to go away in a hurry. There was nevertheless something of a sense of relief.

"We'd better start counting the cost," said Christine Lees. She didn't mean pounds, shillings and pence, although somebody would have to do those sums at some point, but an overview of the likely extent of the damage, including a provisional casualty figure. It would take years to sort out the money issue. Now, there would need to be a statement, she said, and she asked her PR people to keep working on one.

"No detail – just a tight official summing-up for our media friends. You'll have to be vague on a lot of it. The amount of standing water…" Here she caught Caroline's eye, "…is 'several million megalitres'. That's as close as we'll get." Caroline nodded approval. "As for damage," Lees continued, shrugging, "well, it's 'widespread'. We won't be able to get any closer than that until tomorrow morning at the earliest. I'm afraid the number of casualties has reached 27. That's for the whole country, but more reports are still being checked."

Aerial images were now starting to come in from search and rescue as well as news helicopters. Looking at a video clip of the redrawn foothills of the Quantocks, Caroline noticed fields at the edge of the water were much lighter than the higher-up green grass, for all the world as if they had a lace trim. She was about to ask why when she realised she was looking at big groups of cattle, sheep and other animals relocated onto safe dry land.

Saunders was back now, as was Mike Winter, both looking a few shades brighter for their rest and showers. Winter began to help the Environment Agency chief to map all the points where flood banks and barrages had failed in the surge's onslaught. They wanted some idea of the work that would be needed to prevent such a tragedy in the future, should similar circumstances arise. Caroline was still liaising with Connor in Exeter, who had just told her that Miranda thankfully appeared to have diminished to a storm, albeit still a severe one, and that the eastward thrust of the surge had slowed. Nevertheless, that left a mountain of water banked up against the west coast and hemming in everything that had been pushed up the Severn. It might take days for that to dissipate and level itself out with the rest of the Atlantic. She relayed all the news to the team, and then, along with Chief Constable Lees, it was her turn for a rest. Saunders was officially given charge of the operation, while Mike took over her job.

But before sleeping, Caroline telephoned home, wondering if Palfrey had gone to his gallery. She was relieved when he answered.

"That was one terrible storm," he said. "What's it like there? Is everything as bad as they're saying it is?"

"Probably worse. And how's the town coping?"

"Damp," he said, "Very, very damp. The river's a nightmare and downstream, most of the flood banks weren't big enough. There's water everywhere. But no serious local casualties so far, from what I've heard. And the gallery's OK but I've shut shop for the time being. When are you coming back?"

"Not any time soon, I'm afraid. They still want me tomorrow. Anyway, the road's flooded and the rail line's damaged, so I can't come."

"Shall I borrow a pedalo and come and get you?" Palfrey suggested, "I think I can see one coming down the road now."

She laughed.

"I'll ring you tomorrow," she said, "this line's really for emergencies. Bye."

***

Connor at last got his chance to talk on the phone with Saunders.

"I've seen the aerial pictures and I expect you have too," Connor said. "It's as bad as we expected, perhaps even worse. We'll have to get together as soon as we can to put together a report – Prime Minister's orders. As a complication, I must run statements past my boss, Marion Cooper. And the Prime Minister wants at least one of us – perhaps both of us – up in London with her, so that we can add gravitas to any announcements. Can you get to London early in the morning? Are your trains still getting through?"

"I think so," said Saunders. "But the Bristol-Exeter line is a dead duck, so you'll have to avoid that route. I've been doing a few calculations about what might be needed in the way of protection for a future flood like this, and I don't think we should discuss this on the phone. You've got the climate data we both need, haven't you?"

"I have. But look, I'm desperately tired now so I need a couple of hours of shut eye to give the grey matter a rest. I'll check with the station before I go off home, but what say we aim to meet somewhere in London at around 11 o'clock? Not Paddington, because I might miss you among too many people. National Gallery steps? Politicians probably won't even be awake by then, so we'll have an hour or so."

"Is it all right for you to leave Operation Sandbag?" was his next question.

"Very capable hands here – especially your young pair. And my deputy's on his way as I speak. How about you?"

"Michael, there's hundreds of us here, you'd be surprised, more and more every minute. We can hardly move. Plus, I've got a boss here who's very, very worried."

"Oh?"

"People are starting to ask her why there was so little time to prepare for Miranda. She thinks they want a head to roll."

"Oh dear," said Saunders. "They do love a witch-hunt, don't they, especially if it takes minds off their own inadequacies. Not the time to worry now. See you tomorrow. I'll let you know if I can't find a train or if I'm running late."

***

Connor's meeting with Marion Cooper had been difficult right from her opening statement.

"If it comes to the crunch, I will of course offer to resign."

"You can't. It would be like admitting you've done something wrong, which you haven't. And you're the best chief this outfit has had, by far. They can't afford to lose you. A storm this size and the surge were unpredictable, you know that. If we stick to our guns they won't be able to give us any black marks, at least none that will stick."

She looked at him levelly across her desk, then stood, and looked away out through the streaming window.

"Thanks for the vote of confidence. But since when did the truth make any form of defence? If it's a question of my head or the Environment Minister's, I know who I'd put my money on. And, as you know, there are plenty of people, especially government cronies, who would like to be boss of a quango."

She turned back to look at him, and sat down. "They'd have no trouble filling my shoes. And they wouldn't 'let me go' without a few sweeteners, pension, that sort of thing, so I won't be out on the street begging. Think about that. Do you have a better idea?"

He smiled at the thought of her sitting on the pavement with a begging bowl.

"As a matter of fact, I believe I do."

Chapter 19

As the storm clouds spiralled away to the east, there was a collective sigh of relief from most Britons. But it was an anxious time for anyone who had been evacuated from the vast flooded areas of the West of England. Thousands faced the first of several nights away from their homes and livelihoods, and in many instances did not know what they would find when they went back.

By sunset there was hardly a cloud in the duck-egg blue sky to the west of the Chilterns, but across the newly formed inland sea a mist started to rise eerily from the water, at first in little curls and then denser, more universal. Eventually visibility was down to less than 100 yards or so. Although people were still waiting to be pulled from rooftops, rescue boats were called-in for safety's sake and helicopters were grounded.

Almost everybody now had a flood or a storm story of their own. For those who had electricity (and many still did not, all across the country but more so in the west), the TV stations were full of accounts – a truck and its driver swept away, a caravan with a holidaying family floating through fields, and even a hunt for a tiger that had escaped from a flooded zoo cage among them. Nobody would be short of such dramatic tales for some time to come. And it was reported there was a growing 'missing, presumed drowned' list to go with a casualty list of 32 confirmed dead and many hundreds suffering from storm-related injuries.

***

Skipper Colin Roach and his crew had been navigating *Jocasta* cautiously since the really bad weather abated. To get back to Newlyn the boat had to round the Longships Lighthouse at the tip of Land's End, pass Gwennap Head and the Runnel Stone, and then skirt Mousehole and St Clement's Isle before entering Mounts Bay and hopefully finding a safe harbour. But the main reason for slow progress now that they were closer to land was that they had twice hit broad trails of flotsam washed offshore by the storm – mostly tree trunks, some planks, bits of mashed-up boats, chairs, even an upturned table. Some of this rubbish had been half-submerged, and Roach was worried about ploughing into something invisible but hard and breaking a screw. If they were disabled heaven only knew what might happen to them in an area renowned for shipwrecks. To cap it all the mist came and went, sometimes faint, sometimes dense. So, it was go-slow, even though they had a man aboard who very likely needed medical attention. Better safe than sorry – and in any event, things back in the harbour at Newlyn were far from happy. The fishing port had taken a severe knock from Miranda, and was still badly flooded, he learned from shore reports. What was going on in the rest of the country looked worse – widespread flooding, many drowned. A catastrophe, they were calling it.

In spite of the fact that neither he, Pete Walby nor the Nancarrow lad had slept for a while, and the water was now flat enough for easy going, he radioed Harry Cook's son, the acting harbourmaster, to say he thought it was best for them to anchor and hold-off through the night. They would come in with the morning tide when it might be possible to see more clearly.

"Good idea," was the response. "It's still hellish here – water everywhere. And there's drifting boats all over the place so you p'raps wouldn't get through easy. How are your casualties?"

"It's only one of the chaps we pulled out of the sea I'm really worried about," Roach said. "He hasn't come round at all yet. His mate's a bit shivery but OK. The rest of us will live all right though, I reckon."

"Would it help to talk to a paramedic about the unconscious man?"

"Might be useful."

"I'll see if I can arrange that and call you back. But give us a bit of time. You've heard our lifeboat's still out, have you? *Tahiti Girl*'s missing. Nothing heard from her. She wasn't fishing far from you. Did you see anything of her?"

"No!" said Roach, deeply shocked, imagining the 22-foot crabber and her two-man crew, Alan Blake and his 18-year-old son Wayne. He remembered the boat following him out when *Jocasta* had left Newlyn.

"Afraid so. Everyone's worried. Keep your eyes skinned, eh?"

Pete Walby looked at his skipper's shocked face, frowned. Jago Nancarrow also caught the suddenly serious tone of voice and whipped his head around.

"Trouble?"

"*Tahiti Girl* – missing," Roach said aside to his crew. Then, to Newlyn: "We'll be looking out for her as best we can. Let's hope it's just their radio playing up. Let us know if you find them. I don't suppose anyone's checked what happened to *Anita* – the container ship our jolly sailors fell off?"

"Safe and sound just making it into Cork. They got a tow-in. Goodbye for now *Jocasta*."

Roach put the handset down.

"Well, that's one bit of good news, I suppose. But *Tahiti Girl*…" he shrugged, "…we can only hope."

They brought *Jocasta* round to face into a light wind and dropped anchor. When Roach cut the engine a silence fell, save for the lap, lap, lap of water on the side planks. What swell there had been had now dropped away, and the anchor rope hung limply. Roach suggested two-hour watches so that they could all snatch a bit of sleep. Walby took the first.

Because of the wayward mist he had a flashlight and bell to signal their presence in the night to any craft that might be making its way past their position., If the mist grew denser they'd have to give these signals every five minutes or so in the hope they'd be heard or seen, and not run-down.

The off-duty pair tucked themselves into what space was left on the cabin seats.

The last of the light left the sky.

***

John Carter and Tad Morgan had to wade through water calf-deep, carrying their socks and shoes in loaned shopping bags, to get back to the main road in Newnham and climb the hill to reach Tad's car. The road was still crowded with people who, if they weren't just stunned by the events of the morning, seemed to be waiting to see if yet more disasters were on the way.

The police were gathered in the car park by their vehicles, and somebody had brought them tea and bacon rolls. Only the Super was busy, pacing back and forth, ear pressed to his mobile. Everybody was waiting for orders, but as yet directives appeared to be in short supply.

"This is major major, isn't it?" said Tad as they climbed in. "I wonder if Alan Jenkins and co made it. I hope so. They'll have a bit of a tale to tell."

Carter, who had said very little since they left Unlawater House, shrugged. "Impossible to say. They'd have to have been damn lucky. I'll call the police in Gloucester when I get back to the office and see if they know anything. Can you come in and download your stuff? I'll need to get to work straight away on a roundup."

"Don't you want to go home first, see if your wife is back?"

Carter said nothing immediately. From the high ground between Newnham and Blakeney they had occasional views across the extensive flooded land to the west, again viewed in silence. What more could be said? The scale of the inundation was overwhelming. Only when they were winding down the corkscrew hill into Blakeney did he break his silence.

"Okay, yes. I will make a quick check at home, if that's all right with you."

A little while later, as they approached his house, Carter was relieved to see the office car outside. The offside front tyre was clearly flat. Tad drew up and Carter unlocked his front door and went in alone. No sign of life downstairs. "Phil?" he shouted. No response, none of that feeling you get when somebody else is in the house either. Entering the kitchen, he saw his car keys on the table and an envelope with the single word 'John' on the outside. He stuffed it into his pocket without opening it, went back outside and locked the door.

He got back in Tad's vehicle.

"Office," he directed.

Chapter 20

It was an anxious night for anyone worrying about their homes and possessions and, in some cases, their animals. The whole country woke, however, to a bright dawn, and the mist that had risen from the standing water in the night, blanketing everything, started clearing as soon as the sun was up.

Early news reports dashed any hopes that things might suddenly improve, that the waters would start to retreat, and that all would once again be well. The sea level at the coast had stubbornly stayed as high as it was at the zenith of the flood. In fact, by the time the next tide was due in there was no discernible movement up or down. It was as if there had been no low water at all, as if the tides had become stuck.

Television and radio news reports were suggesting that from inquiries made so far at the Operation Sandbag HQ near Bristol, it appeared that so much water from the Atlantic had been pushed into the west coast and along the Channel that it might take 'some time' to properly start running off. The BBC reported it was trying to get senior people from the Met Office and the Environment Agency to come in and explain the situation, but so far, they hadn't been able to contact any bigwigs.

When would it all be gone? Days, possibly weeks was the best answer they could give.

Some reports added there had been instances of looting, both from homes and businesses, and the police were keeping an eye on this situation, in some cases using drones to act as sentries. Anyone who was caught stealing, a police spokesman stated, would face a severe sentence.

A BBC Radio 4 report raised the question of the overall cost – astronomically high, of course, to just make good the damage to homes and businesses, let alone repair breeched flood defences. Even getting unwanted water off the land would be expensive. Again, Portishead was reluctant to put a figure on this – 'Too early to say' – but it was safe to speculate that there would soon be figures ending in lots of noughts flying around.

The government had appropriated the civilian-initiated rescue fund and was promising to top it up, Portishead was glad to report. Nobody would be made homeless by the event 'thanks to the generosity of British people and well-wishers in countries around the world'.

Could it happen again? If so, how soon? Was global warming to blame? Nobody at Operation Sandbag could answer that last query, but a national statement was expected at around 1pm from the Prime Minister, who was now chairing another Cobra meeting.

The BBC ended its report with a quote from a spokesman for the insurance industry. People should check their policies carefully, he said, and if they thought they had a claim they should make contact as soon as possible.

And they managed to slip in a bit of breaking news: the tiger had been recaptured.

***

For the first time in days Colin Roach felt good. The mist had cleared, the sun was shining, Mounts Bay was in sight, and 'round the corner' was his home port. Furthermore, there was the hint of a southerly breeze and the sea was calm – flat as a millpond. Apart from knocks and bruises and Walby's broken finger, *Jocasta*'s crew was tired but otherwise in good shape.

One of the rescued men was sitting up and taking an interest in the world, and the other seemed to be breathing more naturally and had a better colour. Roach had had a brief talk with a paramedic who said that if his vital signs were reasonably OK, he might not be too bad. Best on the whole to try not to wake him but to keep him warm. They were chugging along smartly – a piece of music like that intro they had always played for *The Onedin Line* would make life perfect…

The sight of their first drifting ship – a 20ft 'windbagger' with her sails still furled and a cover still over her outboard – reminded him that *Tahiti Girl* and her crew had not yet been found. Roach needed to check up on that, but first he decided they would take the apparently undamaged boat – *Alison* from Falmouth – in tow rather than leaving it drifting in the shipping lanes. It proved easy to hitch her up with a short rope, and when they were underway again, he called Newlyn.

"*Jocasta*, coming in to you in about an hour with a couple of casualties. And we have a Falmouth sailing boat in tow – looks like she broke her moorings. Is there any news of *Tahiti Girl*?

There wasn't – and the lifeboat was coming in empty-handed after passing over the search to the Air-Sea Rescue helicopter at first light. Other shipping was also on the lookout. Understandably, friends and relatives alike were beside themselves with worry about the fate of the two fishermen.

Jocasta would have to come in 'very careful' the harbourmaster said because the town looked and felt like it had been bombed and most of the quayside was under water still.

"We've almost got you in sight. Best to stay hopeful for *Tahiti Girl*," Roach said before ending the call.

In short order they passed two more drifting unmanned sailing boats and one half-submerged cabin-cruiser. But they couldn't pick up any more so he noted their names and positions and carried on into the bay where they passed yet another empty cabin cruiser and a lot of floating rubbish before they took the final turn for home.

It was easy to see Newlyn had been caught hopping by the tide earlier that morning as it had come in on top of the surge flooding that had still not cleared. Although the sea was quiet now, water was still lapping at the very brink of the long protective harbour arm to their starboard and curling around the light at the tip of the stubby jetty on the port side. A lot of ships' prows and superstructures were clearly visible riding high beyond the harbour walls. What it must have been like with a storm lashing all this he could only guess – terrifying probably.

Colin brought *Jocasta* in close by the starboard wall, where a figure in waders with water up to his calves was waving and pointing him in towards the fish dock. John Cook, Harry Cook's son. The man cupped his hands around his mouth megaphone-like and shouted as they got closer: "Ambulance over at the fish dock. See you round there."

Colin steered round the half-submerged walls at low speed and dropped to a tickover to coast-in at the fish dock. Behind the buildings there was an ambulance, blue lights flashing, and on the dock two paramedics with stretchers and two dock workers waited, up to their ankles in water. Further back on dry ground was Jago Nancarrow's mother among a small group of villagers that included Pete Walby's girlfriend Tessa and his own wife, Jane.

They waved, glad to see him coming in. Further back still was another woman who did not wave. Colin recognised her as Alan Blake's wife.

Nancarrow was over the side first, running to his mother and earning a smothering hug. One of the two sailors from *Anita* was able to step ashore himself, still wearing a blanket around him, and he was escorted to the ambulance. The paramedics came aboard to strap the other man, still unconscious, onto a stretcher to carry him off *Jocasta*. When one of them saw Walby's bandaged finger he asked what it was. When Walby told him it was broken, he too was directed to the ambulance for a ride to Truro hospital.

"Don't leave a broken finger," the paramedic said, "You could lose it easy. And if you lose a finger there's a high risk you'll lose the use of your hand too. It needs to be strapped up properly." Walby turned and waved to his skipper before entering the vehicle. They took Tessa aboard too, shut the doors and the ambulance hurried away, lights flashing.

"Any fish, Col?"

John Cook, who had come around from the harbour arm, put the question. Colin nodded and a man was sent aboard to lift out his three boxes of scallops, the ice just about lasting out.

"I'll come aboard and take you to a space I've got for *Jocasta*. It's getting a bit crowded in here now," John said.

Colin winked at his wife as they set off. "See you in half an hour," he said. "Put the kettle on."

"Will you be swimming up or sailing?" she joked, looking round at the flooded streets behind.

At that moment there was a loud 'toot, toot, toot," from a foghorn and everyone turned to look at the harbour mouth, where the Penlee lifeboat was just coming in.

On the way to the dock space, John told Colin the community was deeply worried about *Tahiti Girl*. "We're all praying, of course, but…"

When they tied up John left, making his way to the lifeboat mooring, while Colin made his way home alone, sloshing through flooded streets.

***

The early train from Bristol to London was an emergency service because regular rolling stock and engines were either in the wrong place because of the floods or had been stranded because of weather-related line and signalling problems. There was very little space; commuters and other travellers were all scanning their phones for information on the disaster. The mood was subdued, almost grim.

The passengers had been told an estimated arrival time but had been warned there could well be delays. Michael

Saunders, leaning against a passageway wall, checked his own phone for the latest news. The situation was much the same as when he had left Operation Sandbag's Portishead HQ earlier – many injuries, extensive property damage, and an updated body count that had now reached 52. A new Cobra meeting was assembling. There was to be a statement from the Prime Minister, to be carried by all media outlets, expected at around 1pm. Messages pledging support from the high and mighty all around the world were pouring in and an emergency fund appeal was already up and running.

Saunders was glad to learn that Mervyn Connor was on his way. He had needed another helicopter hop from Exeter. They were both on-course for their rendezvous. But he was mightily annoyed, as was Connor he later learned because they had both been gagged. Word from on high had come through that they were to make no press statements, other than giving the bare facts, until they had met with the Prime Minister at midday.

As leading scientists in their field, Saunders and Connor had in the past frequently given interviews to the media when matters concerning the weather or the environment had cropped up. Normally they could do so without needing any kind of official sanction. Now they had been told to keep schtum. Innately suspicious of politicians, Saunders feared (as did Connor) there was some sort of malarkey afoot.

On his laptop Saunders had the draft – or to be precise his part of the draft – of the statement he and Connor had been asked to produce for the Prime Minister about where Miranda had come from, why there was such scant notice of her arrival, why she was so destructive, and what measures needed to be taken to prepare for a similar event in the future – should there be any likelihood of that.

On that last matter he and Connor both knew that climate change was the root of the problem, and that large storms, such as Miranda, accompanied by rising sea levels, would undoubtedly be more frequent. So too would flash floods, heatwaves, destructive winds and occasional spells of intense cold like the 'beast from the east' in 2018.

These facts were going to be accompanied by a map, also in Saunders' briefcase, of flood defence work that would be vital to prevent a disaster on a similar scale: new and higher banks, deeper drainage channels, and better barrages at river mouths. The joint conclusion of all this was that Miranda was a wake-up call. The world was warming, polar ice was melting and the seas were rising. It was time to stop just talking about climate change and start taking the matter much more seriously.

***

When his boss, Marion Cooper, had told him she would take the rap and resign over Miranda, if it came to that, Connor had countered with another proposal, one he had been thinking about for some time but which had just come into sharp focus. Like Marion Cooper he was getting more and more exasperated with political inactivity on climate change. No matter how clearly the dangers of global warming were spelled out – together with remedies, of course – nothing happened. Or, if it did, it happened far too slowly to be effectual.

The one big problem that he and Marion Cooper faced was that they were lead players in a quango and were therefore de facto civil servants who were not being paid to rock any boats. Effectively gagged, in fact.

"So, you see," he told her, "it makes far more sense if I resign rather than you. I've got a private pension and since I've become single again, I have few needs and I can take a salary cut. I've long wanted to bang some heads together on the climate issue and this is my big chance to make a bloody nuisance of myself as I go about it. And the media know me as a 'face' better than they know you, I think you'll agree. They'll listen. They'll love the fact that I've quit and my reasons for doing so. The Met and the government might try to turn me into a dangerous maverick, but the media call the real tune these days so that's what counts – poacher turned gamekeeper…or is it the other way around?"

She had frowned at this but nodded.

"Let's see what happens, shall we?" was her only comment, but he was sure he'd scored a point.

***

For Michael Saunders there were a few inexplicable halts on the way from Bristol, but the train arrived at Paddington fairly quickly, much to his relief. After a short tube ride he and Connor shook hands in Trafalgar Square, which was a scene of normality, abuzz with tour groups. It was hard to imagine Britain was in the middle of a major disaster and that London had until a few hours ago been on full flood alert in case the barrage was topped.

Connor told Saunders they had about three quarters of an hour and then they would have to go – the audience was at 12. He led the younger man to a cafe near the gallery's main entrance. Plenty of empty tables. They sat down with flat whites and croissants and compared notes.

Their opinions were, as expected by both men, very similar. They worked on a draft for the PM – a speech of eight minutes maximum was the order. In half an hour they had something slightly longer, so they went through it again, this time just hitting the target.

"Can't really translate this into words, can we?"

Connor had picked up Saunders' map of suggested flood defence work, which was covered with red lines. These were mostly along coasts and estuary shores but there were many inland too. Some were dotted with exclamation marks, as if they held surprises.

"What are those for?" Connor asked, putting his finger on an area that looked as if it was very surprised indeed.

"That's where our embankments and sea walls failed this time round," said Saunders. "Mostly washed away. As we put in the report, 'extensive flood defence repairs will be necessary'.

"An awful lot. What will that cost?"

Saunders held his hands out, palms up. "Anybody's guess. To get back to where they were before the storm, billions of pounds. To add another metre or so to some of them, which would be necessary if sea levels rise to even half that, billions and billions more."

"Are those real figures? Can you tell a Prime Minister that?"

"All right, 'quite a lot of money' then. That's as close as I can get. But even at the best of times it's hard to get a brass razoo out of them for any work."

He shrugged. "We'd better get moving."

Connor emailed a copy of the release to Miss Mastermind and they took a taxi to Downing Street.

***

They were ushered through an iron gate at the head of the street by a policeman and the door to No 10 was opening as if by magic when they approached.

"I think they've seen us coming," whispered Saunders. "Do you think she was watching behind the lace curtains?"

Connor hissed: "Nobody moves a whisker in this street without it being noticed."

Inside, they were led through open doors into the White Drawing Room, where the steely young woman and a grey-suited and bespectacled fair young man with a notebook on his lap were seated in armchairs with their backs to an ornate fireplace. They both rose as the men entered, but the Prime Minister (who this time wore a down-to-earth outfit of light khaki blouson and trousers – stylish, but with hints of battle fatigues) waved the young man back to his seat and came to give welcome handshakes alone.

"Prime Minister," said Saunders stiffly, finding himself bobbing his head in deference. Connor, who was not at all at home with stuffy formalities, merely said a polite "good morning Prime Minister" in return to her "Welcome to Downing Street", which came with a hand gesture to encompass the elegant room. They introduced themselves again, both wondering if she had forgotten what they looked like from the first Miranda Cobra meeting.

She indicated they should sit on the nearest of the two sofas facing her across a coffee table and introduced the young man as Ivor Kemp, who would, she said, "take note of anything you can tell us."

Kemp nodded acknowledgement to them both.

"Now," the Prime Minister said, sitting down herself. "What have you got for us?"

She continued speaking, while Saunders fiddled with the catch on his briefcase and brought out the laptop.

"We are, of course, deeply concerned about this tragedy, or should I call it a disaster? It has taken us all by complete surprise – the whole country, I mean. So many dead – such destruction! I believe it is the worst thing that has happened to this country since the Second World War."

Connor immediately wanted to butt in and remind her of the North Sea Flood of 1953, but she was continuing without a break and he didn't get a chance.

"Now, our Cobra meeting this morning decided that Operation Sandbag was more than capable, a wonderful team. Without them things might have been so much worse. But now it's my job to address the nation, tell them we're doing everything in our power to help everyone affected, reassure them.

"That's why I've asked you both here. I need all the salient facts at my fingertips, from the experts' mouths."

She sat back. Saunders had placed his laptop on the table and opened it. "We were asked to prepare a speech..." he started to say, but she put up a hand to stop him.

"Quite so – and you have?"

"If we could access a printer?"

Again, this was waved away.

"Not necessary. Is that your presentation there? Can I see it please?"

The two men had quizzical looks for each other as Saunders turned the computer round for her and moved it across the table.

"Mr Kemp," the PM addressed the young man who had so far done little more than smile, "come behind me and look this over. Take notes as we go. I'll indicate what I want."

She leant forward, drew the machine closer and read while the two men sat in silence and her note-taker dutifully rose and went to look over her right shoulder. Now and then she nodded, sometimes she shook her head, and quite often she pointed at something for the benefit of the young man alone. There were few audible comments – "We'll need that," was one, and "I don't think we can say that," was another, but mostly double jabs at the screen with her forefinger and a quick glance over her shoulder got the young shorthand-writer scribbling away.

She went over it once – a quick reader – and scrolled back to the start to take another look.

"Good,", she said eventually, looking up at them. "I don't think you've missed a thing. Very thorough. Thank you both very much. I hope you can leave this…" she indicated the laptop, "…with us for the time being – is that all right? I'll see it gets back to you at your headquarters in…"

"Bristol," Saunders filled in for her. "Not far from the Operation Sandbag HQ actually. No, of course you can have it, but we…er…we were rather thinking you might want to talk over some of the content with us. We…"

But he got no further – she was gesturing for him to stop. Checking her watch, she turned to the young man and said: "Ivor, take this and start right away on it, will you please? Oh, and get someone to make sure we send Mr Saunders' machine back to him, will you?"

When Kemp had left the room, she said, "He's my speech writer. He's a quick worker and he knows what I want. Now, discussion – is there anything left to talk about, Mr Saunders? Well, I'm afraid we're out of time for anything like that, but I ought to tell you both that this announcement is a very important one. Principally, it must reassure the nation rather than frighten them. That's how I see my job, you see. I appreciate all your points about storm frequencies and global warming, but now is not the time to raise these subjects. They'll just worry people. Which is why I've asked both of you to avoid talking with the media on these matters, important though they are, for the time being. Be deliberately vague, if you like, if you get direct questions, but above all avoid scaring people.

"All sorts of things hinge on that – soaring insurance premiums, falling house prices, and demands for better flood prevention measures, and above all expenses which we haven't even guessed at yet. Alarms – not that I'm calling either of you alarmist, that is – alarms can have unexpected consequences. Let us get over this crisis and then we can turn our attention to all that. Can I get your word of honour on this, both of you please?

Was she right? Connor swallowed. Both he and Saunders knew that Britain, as well as the rest of the world, was on the brink of a disaster. Most of the dramatic effects of global warming had occurred in the past ten years and were going on occurring with increasing frequency. Governments needed to get to grips with this now, at this very moment, but they remained obstinately tardy. If they had been faced with war, mountains would have been moved by now. Yet the implications they were facing were in a way far more serious than war.

The frustrations for people like him and Saunders in the face of a 'there are more important matters to deal with' attitude were almost unbearable. Why was so little being done? When would the message get through? He looked at Saunders. He must be thinking much the same way as I am, he thought, yet here we both are being asked by this young woman to hold back, to reassure rather than sound warnings. And, of course, she headed the government that paid their wages: She paid the pipers; she called the tune.

He nodded slowly; Saunders followed suit. She raised her eyebrows: it had to be said.

"We will try not to scare the horses, Prime Minister," said Connor. "You have our word."

It earned a rare smile from her. Another watch check, then she stood up and said briskly: "Well, I haven't much time left so I must move on but thank you both once again for your cooperation. It has been a great help. But can I ask you, Mr Connor, to stay for a minute for a private word? You, Mr Saunders, may wait in the hallway if you wouldn't mind. I'm afraid you haven't got clearance to stay outside with the Press for my speech, but there are places nearby where you can watch it on television and it'll probably be streamed on your phones."

They two men were both on their feet now. The door out of the room had opened magically, reinforcing Connor's feeling that everything was being closely monitored in this seat of power. Saunders, puzzled, bobbed again and left. They watched him go, then the PM turned.

"I am sorry to have to ask you this, Mr Connor, but was there any prior indication of Storm Miranda that might have been overlooked? I suppose I'm asking if there was any way we might have learned it was on its way earlier? I know you people don't rely on looking at bunches of seaweed anymore, but surely there must have been some way of seeing it coming sooner. Satellite imaging, that sort of thing? And haven't you just got a new supercomputer? People are asking, you see."

Connor felt a sudden icy chill running down his spine. Was this the start of the inquest, the 'witch hunt' Saunders had hinted at?

He nodded. "Yes, we do rely mostly on interpreting satellite information, but in this instance, we've run the sequence back and there was very little indication the storm would develop so quickly and be so destructive. Just a slight atmospheric disturbance, that's all, off the coast of America. Probably a remnant hurricane that had dwindled to almost nothing. We see them all the time, and usually in terms of our weather they're quite insignificant. The time to sound the alarm was when it combined with another growing depression at exactly the same moment as the highest tide in an age – and I think we showed due diligence on moving swiftly after that."

She was quiet for a moment. then: "And who exactly monitors these storms? I know the Met Office has a large staff. Is there constant surveillance?"

"Yes." Connor, hands at his sides, felt himself making fists.

"But, overall, is that your responsibility, or would it be your CEO's – Marion Cooper, isn't it?"

He shook his head. "Marion's role is largely supervisory. I'm in charge of the monitoring and I oversee the forecasting – and I'm the PR front man. But I really don't think anyone in my department, anyone at all, can be held responsible for the short notice on Miranda."

"I see. Well, we'll leave it at that Mr Connor. I'm not asking anyone to take responsibility for that now, nor am I asking anyone to consider their position, so we'll say goodbye. And I really do appreciate all the work you've done on material for the announcement. Thank you."

She was holding out a hand. The smile was no longer present.

"Goodbye."

When he left the room, almost tripping over a woman hurrying in with a tray of make-up materials and brushes, he found he was shaking from head to foot. This shocked Saunders in the hall but not the doorman. He had seen people leave that room in far worse states.

When they exited into a still-bright day, a lectern was being set up in the road in front of the house, and the press were gathering, setting up tripods, testing cameras, some already on-air talking to listeners or viewers. Someone in the press gang who knew Connor waved and shouted his name, but he was tight-lipped until they left the street and the iron gate clanged shut behind them.

Then he said: "Let's find a bar Mike. I need a strong drink."

Chapter 21

TV viewers who had been waiting with eager, if trepid, anticipation for the Prime Minister's announcement saw the two men leaving the front door of No 10 and walking briskly away, ignoring a shout of "do you have anything to say Mr Connor?" from one of the reporters.

Two minutes later, the door opened again, and the PM emerged, notes in hand. Taking the papers to the stand she held them down with one hand and began: *"People of Britain, I want to commend you all for your bravery and courage on this very grave situation. In the terrible flooding and storms that have affected almost the whole country, but especially the South West, nearly 100 people have died and many more have been injured, while some – especially those at sea – are still unaccounted for. The damage to property is extremely serious and widespread. Some of the floodwaters will take days if not weeks to dissipate.*

"Throughout all this Britain's emergency services, as well as citizens like yourselves, have worked tirelessly, some for more than 24 hours non-stop, to try to ensure everyone is safe. Without all your brave efforts the casualty list from Storm Miranda would have been immeasurably worse. Despite the short notice of the storm's arrival, we are pleased to say

Operation Sandbag has been an enormous success in preventing an even greater tragedy.

"Now it is time to start the clear-up. I first want to assure anyone made homeless by Miranda that they will be rehoused at the earliest opportunity, and we as a government will spend what it takes to clean-up and restore flooded properties, especially for those not fully covered by insurance. We will be helped, of course, by the very generous contributions to the growing relief fund: contributions from sympathisers around the world as well as here at home. An enormous effort.

"I would like to urge anybody who thinks they can help the situation in any way whatsoever to contact the emergency telephone number which will be given at the end of this broadcast. There is also a number for people who have been unable to contact relatives or friends in the main flood areas.

"I have this morning spoken with Environment Agency chief Michael Saunders, who is monitoring the flood water and whose staff are all urgently engaged in taking the levels down. Mr Saunders assures me every effort will be made to restore damaged flood defences, and to this end my Government has pledged another billion pounds to be spent over the next five years. Power-line teams are also working around the clock, and I praise the patience of those waiting for their electricity to be restored.

"I have also spoken this morning with Mervyn Connor who heads the monitoring section of the Meteorological Office. He tells me Storm Miranda took everyone by surprise with her sudden arrival, her strength and her ferocity – but events such as these, with a high tide and a storm surge coinciding, are fortunately very rare. We hope we do not see Miranda's like again, and we also hope we can have better warning of extreme weather events in the future.

"Storm Miranda was a big shock for us all, but now I am asking everyone to buckle down and do whatever is necessary for our recovery, led by this government.

"The Dunkirk spirit saw us all through the worst days of World War Two. I know the Dunkirk spirit is alive and well in Britain today.

"Thank you once again, one and all."

Connor looked at Saunders. They were on their second pint. Somebody had switched the television off and hubbub had returned to the pub.

"Shall I fall on my sword now, or shall I wait to see if it all quietens down?" the Met man said.

Saunders patted him on the shoulder. "Wait and see – always best. I'd suggest another drink, but we'd be piddling all the way home. You'd better come to Paddington with me. I doubt if they've paid for a helicopter home for you, have they?"

Connor shook his head.

"I'm well out of being any more use now I would guess."

***

John Carter had been waiting for the text of the Prime Minister's speech to finish off his flood edition *Clarion*. Once that was done and dusted and off to still-flooded South Wales for printing, he opened the envelope Phyllis had left and took out the single sheet of notepaper with a sinking heart.

"*Dear John.*" How many letters have started like that, he wondered to himself?

"*I am sorry I had to leave so suddenly, but I have been feeling so lonely since your job became so much to you that it took up most of the time. I am afraid that, for me at least, it is not enough just to sleep together. When we married, I thought we would have more time together, not less – and I also thought we might have babies, or at least one, and 'raise a family' as they say in the films. The trouble is, I still love you very much, so I am going away to think about all this – I cannot tell you where or for how long. I hope you will think about it too. I will let you know when I am back – probably at my old home in Bath. Well, goodbye for now – do look after yourself please. With love, Phyllis XXX*"

***

It was the day after that when he got a chance to talk with battered maverick bore-rider Alan Jenkins, recovering in hospital in Gloucestershire Royal since being plucked out of a muddy field at Framilode. He took him some fruit and a paper.

"Hello Johnno!"

He was surprisingly chipper for a man with a fractured arm and smashed ligaments in his right calf, although the bandaged head looked suitably piratical. The hospital staff had made him sit up in a chair beside his bed, and Carter had to bring a plastic chair from a stack to sit facing him.

"They were going to chuck me out soon as they'd strapped me up, but they got worried about sepsis or some new thing like that," he said. "An' they thought I perhaps swallowed too much dirty water than was good for me. Tried to tell them I drink it all the time, but they wouldn't listen. What's the world like out there? Still flooded it looks from the telly pictures."

"It is," agreed Carter. "Still pretty bad too – and nobody can say how long it will take to put it all to rights. Here…" He plonked a large bunch of grapes in a paper bag on Jenkins' bed, noticing as he did so that more fruit as well as boxes of chocolate covered the top of the bedside cabinet. "If you get many more of those, you'll be able to start making wine. Oh, and here's my flood edition."

He put the rolled paper he'd been carrying under his arm in Jenkins' good hand, and the man shook it out to look at the front page composite of pictures – the boarders standing on the bank, three tiny spots heading into a maelstrom surrounded by floods that seemed to stretch all the way to Arlingham on the far bank, and a bold headline, JINKIN' JENKINS DEFIES DEATH, and a sub-head, 'One killed, one missing in Severn Bore tragedy'.

Jenkins grinned, then grimaced because that made his head wound hurt. "'Jinkin' Jenkins' – I like that." Then, suddenly more serious, "I'm sad about old Pete Knapp, though. He was one of the best. His missus is in a terrible state. Should've stayed single like me and Cec, played the field like. Has there been any word on Cec?"

Carter shook his head. He'd heard nothing. Both he and Jenkins knew that the Severn could hide bodies for days, even weeks on end. In normal times they would go downriver with the ebbing tide then come back upstream again when the water rose on the next tide, and could indeed go tens of miles back and forth, back and forth, if they did not rise to the surface. So long as they stayed intact.

"You were dead lucky to get out alive. You know that, don't you?"

Jenkins nodded. "Dead lucky. Is that what you want to tell your readers?"

"More or less. Do I get an exclusive?"

"You're first, but I think the BBC are coming this afternoon. I'll have to talk to them, but I reckon you'll have all the background to make a better story – and the great pictures Tad took from the bank and Unlawater. That's next week's edition taken care of for you."

"I guess. So, what was it like?" asked Carter, taking his notebook out of his pocket.

"Well, like being in a cement-mixer, really – one of those really big ones they have on trucks."

Carter started to write, for the moment forgetting his own problems...

***

Three days after Miranda's visit the leaden skies cleared completely and the forecasters promised a long balmy summer spell that might start to cheer Britain up a bit.

The day after that, Owen James got the call he'd been waiting for from his local NFU rep in Worcester about relief milking – except it wasn't quite the proposition he'd been expecting.

"Hello Mr James, Rhodri Morgan from the NFU – about your recent offer of help over the flood crisis. How many acres of pasture do you have?"

Wondering what on earth that had to do with tearing off to help some flood-hit dairyman, Owen nevertheless replied straight from his thoughts: "Well, let's see. There's the 80 acres down to the river under my kitchen window, and off the bottom corner there's a gate through to eight acres more – tups are in that now. Up the valley we've got roughly 30 acres with the ewes on it. All the lambs are about to go out to be reared-on. Why do you ask?"

"So, you could take 40 milking Friesians, say, plus a portable farmyard milking bail? We'll supply any extra fodder needed. Farmers up and down the country are being very generous."

"You mean you want me to take-in a dairy herd? Here?"

"If you can please. They're a fine bunch of pedigree beasts but they have to be moved on from a holding yard. They're cramped up and anxious and they haven't been looked after properly for the last three or four days, so they need some space to settle themselves down – and regular milking, or they'll be ruined. Can you help? Their owner's going spare. It's going to take a month or more to get the water off his land and even more to bring the pasture back into shape. There'll be money from the compensation fund if you need it."

The cows arrived in two big cattle trucks that very afternoon – Owen had heard the animals bellyaching from miles away as they were driven up the lane. Yet when the truck tailgate was lowered in the yard, with the open gate to the empty pasture wide open before it, there was stunned silence from the herd, and no movement.

"Come on ladies," said Owen. "This is your new home for a bit."

In the end he had to get Meg to pop in among them and ease them out. With tails twitching, the now very dusty black and white cows still did not move far across the cobbles, sniffing the air and looking around with deep suspicion.

With one truck empty, the other one took its place. This lot came out more easily, perhaps because their sisters were already in the yard, but once out they too would not go forward. However, as soon as the trucks had gone, Owen enlisted Alice and Meg's help to get the reunited herd moving reluctantly forward into the sunny green field, where they spread out side by side and stopped again, as if amazed by their surroundings. Owen could see that most of them really needed milking, the sooner the better.

"Lost tribe surveying the promised land do you think?"

The new voice at his elbow came from the cows' owner, a short, almost bald middle-aged man in blue overalls. He introduced himself as David Cunliffe.

Owen laughed. "They certainly do look a bit lost. I think we should leave them alone, just for an hour or so, to settle in – then I've got to see about getting hold of the milking bail the NFU promised."

"Got it with me," said Cunliffe. "Towed it behind my Range Rover. It's out there in the lane, blocking the way I dare say. We'd better get it in and set it up. It takes six animals at a time – and you'll be happy to know it has its own petrol generator. I've brought fuel for it too."

"You'll come to the house for tea first," Alice insisted after he'd pulled the rig in. "The cows will look after themselves for now."

The story that weary-looking David Cunliffe told was not an unusual one. Several generations of his family had farmed the ground he owned near Upton, and there had never been a problem like this before so far as he knew. It was flat pasture and not far from the Severn, but even before they put up flood embankments his fields only got lying water here and there in the very worst winter weather. Now most of them had gone under a good two and a half feet. Luckily the farm buildings, including the milking parlour, had been built on raised ground and he still had road access, so he'd been able to muddle through after the flood until now, keeping his stock in the yard.

"Unhappily, some of the banking they put in twenty or so years ago is almost too good. With the river still up to the top of the barriers it can't run away off my land. It won't soak in, not with all the rain we've had to saturate everything. My animals have always been on pasture for the maximum amount of time possible. They don't know what's hit them now. If it wasn't for you and the NFU I don't know what me and the missus would do. Split the herd and sell up, maybe – that's crossed my mind."

The milking bail was brand-new, straight from the manufacturer, and it had a list of assembly instructions as long as your arm. Nevertheless, they quickly got the mostly-metal contraption ready for the evening milking. It had been a matter of 'all hands on deck', including Alice, to unfold its various parts and tighten up nuts and bolts and, once the non-slip flooring was steady, they could run the piping and electrics through, put the glass collection jars in place and start-up the generator. Now all they needed was the cows.

From being dumbstruck animals, the Friesians had spread themselves out in a broad front across the field and were descending by degrees towards the river, snatching up tussocks here and there as they went on an exploratory trip. Owen, Cunliffe and Meg walked down together to call them in. Owen was explaining the state of his grass, which looked lush and green.

"I've taken a bit of hay from it, but it's coming back fast after all that rain. There may not be a lot of goodness in it yet, but I expect they're glad of it after all that dry food they've had. May give them the runs a bit, though."

He was watching Cunliffe closely. Just like his cows, the man appeared to be very taken with his new surroundings.

"Beautiful, eh?" Owen said softly as he followed Cunliffe's gaze to the high tops with their wooded caps, the paddocks rolling steeply to the river, the pattern of regimented orchard trees here and there, and a bit of plough that looked as if it had been combed. "I sometimes feel I'm the luckiest man alive looking round at all this."

Cunliffe laughed. "I'd say you are. I sometimes think the same about my patch of ground. Although it's mostly flat with just the Malverns poking through, it has its charms, especially the big skies. And then I suppose like you, I come home to the bills on the doorstep and endless paperwork to make me feel grumpy again."

"I'll say."

Cunliffe insisted in mustering his animals by turning round a large nearly all-black cow and encouraging her to head back uphill again. He then walked ahead of her shouting "Hup! Hup!" and the others fell trustingly into line behind the matriarch.

It wasn't quite so simple putting them through the unfamiliar bail but they managed the task, albeit slowly, ending long into twilight. As Owen had surmised, a lot of the animals were glad to lose their burdens, and when they were released back into the paddock they gave heels-up kicks and jumps of joy.

There remained but one big problem. What would they do with the milk?

Cunliffe had brought along enough old-fashioned milk churns for an evening and a morning milking, and despite the offer of a bed for the night he insisted he would drive home and bring back a large trailer milk-tank in time to help in the morning.

"The idea is, I take the milk straight to the dairy – no collections doing the rounds while this flap's going on," he said. "I expect a lot will go to the cheese-makers – lower price, but it can't be helped. Most of the flood-hit farms are in the same way and it will be a long time before things get back to normal. Like I said, without you, don't know what I'd have done. If there are any extra costs..."

Owen waved away any suggestion of payment from a fellow farmer in dire straits.

"Glad to help, really," he said just before the man drove off, "nice to have a new challenge."

Although it was late, he insisted on an over-the-gate check on the sheep up the lane. Back home and in bed later he confided to Alice: "I really like working with cows again," before falling immediately into a deep sleep.

Chapter 22

The next time Mervyn Connor and Michael Saunders met was over lunch at the County Hotel in Taunton, a 'halfway house' between their respective HQs in Exeter and Bristol. It was five days post-Miranda. Like most people affected directly or indirectly by the disaster, they were talking about their future.

"So, you're really feeling up against it now?" said Saunders. "You don't think it will soon all blow over, if you'll excuse the meteorological allusion?"

Connor was shaking his head before his words were finished.

"I don't, Mike. I know in many ways we're very similar, heading these big departments, but I just can't go on sitting on my hands when things are coming to a head like they are. Sorry, I didn't mean to imply you were sitting on your hands in any way – I know you're not. It's more to do with the fact that the climate crisis is much bigger – global, in fact – than Britain's flood defences and drainage problems, serious though they may be."

He tugged his beard while Saunders digested this, then continued: "I know our problems are interlinked, and as kingpins in quangos we have to toe the government line, since they pay our salaries, but that means we've been gagged, and gagged very effectively. And this really isn't the time for a leading meteorologist to hold his tongue. I need freedom to speak my mind. Ha!"

He laughed cynically. Saunders was about to speak, but Connor continued.

"I know you can fight your battles from within. I mean, I know you *will* fight your battles from within – but if you speak out of turn and get sacked they'll find a yes-man to take your place. Me ... well, I've got a good scientific standing in meteorology and I can use that. The media might think initially I'm just falling on my sword for shortcomings in storm warnings, but I've got a whole lot more than that to tell them..."

"You're *leaving*?" Saunders was taken aback. "What about your CEO? Surely, she should be the one to go, your leader?"

"Miss Mastermind? We've discussed it."

"And?"

"And she agrees with me. Gave me her blessing in fact, and that's not simply because it avoided her losing her head. Somebody without government shackles needs to be out there – her words, not mine. If anybody can keep drumming home the climate messages to the powers that be, it has to be me. It's not the execution it might seem, anyway. I take a half-pension, and there are a growing number of jobs with the climate protest movements I could well fit into."

Saunders looked thoughtful. "I suppose that's true. And another truth is that the battle for more spending on flood relief measures can only be made from inside the agency. Only I don't have to convince the government alone because the rest of the country doesn't take much notice of the things we're responsible for either unless something goes wrong. This disaster has been a wake-up call for them. In a sense, it makes my job a lot easier. This time they'll have to do something."

Connor nodded. "Same goes for me."

***

When the next edition of the Clarion came out it was eagerly snapped up. The first-person story 'HOW I

SURVIVED KILLER WAVE' was a great draw, along with some more of Tad Morgan's flood pictures, plus a new one of the hero of the tale, Alan 'Jinkin' Jenkins, smiling from ear to ear and all strapped-up in hospital.

It was a good yarn, even if a little poetic embellishment had been used here and there, such as: "...then a huge shoal of enormous salmon appeared in a wall of water, staring out at me, looking surprised as I was," and "you just don't fight water when its moving fast as an express train, you let yourself go with it" (perhaps a little nearer the truth).

Maybe the most telling phrase of all came at the very end, in the transcript of a mini-interview when the reporter concluded with the question: "I suppose this is the end of your bore-riding days."

Grinning Jack's reply? "I'll be back. Try and stop me."

Ever since Phyllis had left him, John Carter had been putting off the question of his own future while he dealt with the storm and its devastating local effects. Now that he had more time to think, the only conclusion he could come to was that he needed to spend more time with his wife, assuming he could get her back, and perhaps think about starting a family.

Times were not easy for many local newspapers, especially small 'frees' like the Clarion. Many were one man bands editorially with just one journalist like himself 'filling the gaps between the ads' and undertaking all the week-to-week writing tasks from council meetings to sport fixtures, plus anything out of the ordinary that came along, like Miranda. He'd enjoyed it all but, yes, Phyllis was right – he did not see much of her. Not enough, anyway. And he hadn't taken a holiday, just the odd day off, for as long as he could remember.

"They're taking advantage of you," had been her frequent complaint, and, "You're entitled to holidays, you know."

With another edition starting to come together, he dropped it all and, full of resolve, started to write a letter:

"Dear Phil, I'm sorry I have given you a rotten time. I'm going to tell the management that I need some assistance, make more time for myself, for us ..."

***

The rest of the press – all the media in fact – was saying that in terms of overall damage to businesses and livelihoods the cost of the storm was possibly incalculable. Thousands and thousands of agricultural acres had been submerged and much of it was still underwater days later. In cases like David Cunliffe's Upton farm, where floodwater was trapped on the land, it would be weeks before all the water moved away (if it didn't rain again, that is). His pasture would then take a month or more to recover, and that's if it didn't need re-seeding altogether. Arable crops were already ruined in many places, in particular the Severn Vale, parts of South Wales and on the Somerset Levels. More than 3,000 valuable farm animals had perished, either drowning because their owners had not been able to move them away from danger quickly enough or stampeding in panic into deeper and deeper water. Many farmers and other country-dwellers, the people of whole villages and large parts of towns had had to abandon their flooded homes, many not having time to rescue belongings and equipment. Much of that was now ruined. Along with flooring, most electrical white goods that had gone under water had been rendered useless.

The media seemed to relish the ongoing inquest into the cause and effect of the disaster. The body-count in particular – the measure of most tragedies and the stuff of headlines – seemed to obsess people the most, although at 168 storm-related deaths for the whole country it was low compared with the estimated 2,000 killed in the 1607 storm-surge flood. And a week after the event there were still three people missing, presumed drowned – two Newlyn crab-fishermen, a father and son, whose boat *Tahiti Girl* had been found drifting and empty, and a luckless Severn Bore-rider (again, no sign of a body or even a board).

So, apart from *'Fishing community in mourning'* (Newlyn) and *'Prayers at Severn surfers' church'* (Newnham) it appeared the country had got off reasonably lightly – thanks in no small measure, some said, to prior warning from the 'weather boffins' at the Met Office. However, the query had been raised in some quarters that had the warning come earlier, might some of those lost still be alive? And it was a question (though not the only big question) that would not go away.

Asked in a TV interview if there might have been some earlier sign that Miranda was on her way, 'Miss Mastermind', who had now assumed the mantle of the Met's spokesperson on this subject since Connor had tendered his notice (or been 'axed', according to some newspapers), gave the possibility some weight by agreeing with interviewers that yes, there had been signs of a residual west-bound hurricane waiting in the wings around about a day earlier than the storm warning.

Was it overlooked, then, this brewing hurricane?

"We get a few of these, mostly not amounting to much. But yes, I suppose we could have watched it more closely. With hindsight. We have tightened our procedures."

Whose responsibility would missing an approaching storm be? Yours?

"We have a huge department constantly monitoring the weather around Britain – around the world in fact – headed by our chief scientists. They are 99.9 percent accurate most of the time."

But not on this occasion?

"I suppose not."

Then came another leading question: *Is there any likelihood of it ever happening again?*

A guarded answer: "These events are very rare, so far."

And the last of the big questions: *There is a lot of talk about global warming having a big impact on storms – their frequency and ferocity. Is that a view the Met Office shares?*

"The government has set some very tough CO_2 emission targets and if we adhere to these, we can stop temperatures rising so quickly. The rest of the world will have to set similar targets, of course."

***

"Didn't exactly answer the question there, Miss Mastermind," Connor said to himself as he watched the interview at home. He was not yet fully released from his Exeter HQ duties, but he knew he would soon have his turn to speak his mind.

But how did one save the world from this apparently accelerating disaster?

The forces that were driving global warming were well known, and the science behind it was sound. For example, unless we give up our cherished fossil-fuel driven cars and power stations, shift industry and homes over to sustainable electricity, take fewer (or no) air trips, eat far less meat and have far fewer babies, the global jacket of (mainly) carbon dioxide stopping Planet Earth from losing any body heat to outer space will continue to grow – the upshot, Earth will just get hotter and hotter.

This was no longer a projection: global warming was happening, here and now, and its rapidly worsening effects were obvious: bigger and more frequent storms like Miranda and America's hurricanes and the typhoons and cyclones of the East, droughts, crop failures and blazing forests, melting polar ice and rising sea levels – worrying topsy-turvy weather patterns just about everywhere. To deny it was more than crazy; it bordered on criminal.

There were many voices pointing this out. Things were starting to change for the better, sure, but far too slowly to escape increasing climate problems, Connor could see. At this pace, the world was in for some big shocks.

Why the reluctance of the powers that be to move any faster? Why the holding back? Could it be that the sociological changes needed really are just too big to coax a voting public into a brave new world?

Connor couldn't see himself let alone others trying to persuade Mrs X in Bombay not to have another baby, or banning all but electric cars. But he could feel hope, and the hope was in this: he sensed a groundswell of endeavour among young people across the globe to start saving the world they will inherit, to stop its climate going crazy, to preserve its rare and beautiful creatures and diverse flora. Could he help that endeavour? He hoped so, and that was why he wrote to the headquarters of the lead environmental movements to ask if he could be of any use to them.

***

By August, things were changing rapidly at the Met's Exeter HQ. Mervyn Connor was on his way out, even if he still put in an occasional appearance. Rumours were rife that he had joined one of the leading environmental pressure groups – organisations such as this were growing in stature day by day. Who could blame him? He was following his conscience, and he had enough clout to make people sit up and listen to him. The Met's titular CEO, 'Miss Mastermind' Marion Cooper, had survived what everybody was calling a 'witch hunt' virtually unscathed after taking some fancy steps. She had divided Connor's former post into two new jobs, Early Warning Officer and PR/Spokesman, and she had also created a whole new department, titled Projections, to forecast the ifs and buts of global warming and warn of its consequences in a calm and detailed way. She was therefore edging the Met into the area where Connor would be working, and although for him the new positions had come too late, he would not have wanted to go back to the restrictions of being in thrall to government paymasters. 'Projections' would in time, Connor sensed, come in for a lot of interference from the government even if its claims were backed by science and thoroughly researched. Marion Cooper would have to be tough about all this with political leaders. And she would need the cooperation of the Environment Agency to identify measures that might be needed for every degree of temperature rise, and both agencies would have to back each other up. When necessary Connor would be backing them up too – and his hands would no longer be tied, thank goodness.

***

Mike Winter, the man who had first clapped eyes on Storm Miranda, landed one of the jobs in Projections, and it was thought he might in time make his way to the top of the department, so long as it survived. He was quite glad he was not an Early Warning Officer because, as his former colleague Caroline Cleaver reminded him, "isn't there always going to be an occasion when you can't warn everybody early enough?"

When she made that remark, Mike was just packing up his things to move to another area of the HQ, although by sharing key roles in the storm debacle they had become even firmer friends then before. He'd just turned down her offer of teaching him how to knit.

"What is it, anyway?" he said, looking at the still-growing but shapeless multi-coloured tapestry her needles were clacking away at. She shrugged.

"I don't really know. It was going to be a jumper when I started out but it sort of lost that purpose somewhere along the way. I might end up calling it a work of art, and put it in for the Turner Prize – 'Storm Miranda' could be an appropriate title, don't you think? Are you sure you don't want to learn yourself – good for the soul, good for the mind, good for idle hands? Dead simple, look – left over right, make a loop, pull the wool through, right over left…"

She clattered into another row. He shook his head, slowly.

"I haven't got the patience for that I'm afraid, Car. Besides, we'll be very busy, it all being so new."

"It's not that they're all manly types who might not like to have a knitting wimp among their numbers?" she teased.

Caroline, plus her knitting, was staying put in the old department, monitoring the weather patterns, preparing charts and bulletins on Britain's generally fickle but, by and large, benign atmospheric shifts. Going up a notch in grading and a pay boost were welcome bonuses, but these did not matter because she enjoyed the usually quiet, methodical nature of her work, especially at night. It was very much like knitting, in a way.

***

Letter to *The Times* newspaper Saturday August 30:

Sir – On Monday and Tuesday of this week, I was amazed to see large numbers of frogs, tiny to adults, crossing my garden which until two months ago had been completely submerged. I have no idea what this mass movement was about, but by Wednesday there was not one frog to be seen. They had melted into the landscape without trace. Have any other readers had a similar experience I wonder? – Michael Rich, Watchet, Somerset.

***

Later that autumn, police were called to a North Cornwall beach to investigate wreckage that had been washed ashore. They found a battered, empty shipping container and, as it was of no use to anyone, it was cut up there and then and the pieces were carted off to a scrapyard.

If the investigating officers had been more sharp-sighted, they might have noticed that almost all the people in the clifftop village above the bay wore fashionable brand-new Brazilian leather shoes.

THE END

You might also enjoy these books by Ted Lamb:

Match of the Day (Kindle E-book) A coming of age story set against the background of Britain's 1960 Football World Cup campaign.
Gansalaman's Gold (Kindle E-book) Strange disappearances in Dracula country.
The Prophet and the Pelicans (Kindle E-book, paperback) What lies behind one of the oddest books in the Bible? Did prophet Ezekiel actually witness a time-tripping flight of combat helicopters many years before the birth of Christ?
Brassribs (Kindle E-book, paperback) Two generations of anglers have sought Brightwell Lake's biggest carp – but the book also tells of wartime bravery, romance and skulduggery.
Looking for Lucie (Kindle E-book, paperback) Lucie is a very, very big pike – yet while fanatical angler Mark Kendal is trying to catch her, his world is falling apart. What happens when the adversaries finally meet?
Gobblemouth (Kindle E-book, paperback) A 'problem' catfish that has to be rehomed is behind this madcap road-trip across Europe to the River Danube.
The Brightwell Trilogy (Kindle E-book, paperback) The above three books – **Brassribs, Looking for Lucie** and **Gobblemouth** – are contained in this bumper edition.
Monty and the Mauler (Kindle E-book for children) Ace reporter Monty the terrier gets his canine pals together to solve a local mystery
The Fisher's Tale (Kindle E-book, paperback) Walking the pilgrim trail from France to Spain's Santiago de Compostela in 2003.
Ted Lamb (b1944) has been a writer and journalist in Britain and Australia all his working life and his books reflect a keen interest in sport fishing, natural history and travel. He lives in Cheltenham, England.

Printed in Poland
by Amazon Fulfillment
Poland Sp. z o.o., Wrocław